I0555697

SUMMER BY THE JEWEL SEA

RHONDA FORREST

Valeena Press

For all the wonderful friends we've made -
by the Jewel Sea.

For your enjoyment - Sample chapters from 'Silkworm Secrets'
are in the back of this book. Happy reading!

WHITSUNDAY ROMANCE

Enjoy the warmth of a small community in the Whitsundays.
You may never want to leave!

~~~

Love by the Jewel Sea - Book 1
Summer by the Jewel Sea - Book 2
The Lure of the Jewel Sea - Book 3

DON'T MISS OUT ON THESE BOOKS!

*** If you enjoy a mixture of small town stories, the Australian Outback, and romance, make sure to read - Queensland Outback Romance Series

SUMMER BY THE JEWEL SEA

CHAPTER 1

*F*rankie clenched her teeth, her hands grasping her swollen stomach. The back seat of the small sedan was hard and narrow under her back and she yelled at Simon to drive faster, put his foot down... and she inhaled sharply – her next words lost as stabbing pains ripped across her belly – bloody drive like there was no tomorrow because it felt like this baby was coming now!

Rolling onto her side, she closed her eyes, the discomfort easing slightly as she pushed her face into the seat. When she gulped for air, the agony returned, gripping her body like a vice. She curled her legs up next to her, hoping that it would all go away; that the pain wouldn't come back and the clenching spasms tearing across her torso would disappear.

Her stomach was tight, an enlarged hard ball of stretched muscles that had protected and held her and Simon's first baby, safely, for the last eight months. This delivery part wasn't supposed to happen yet. She should have another four weeks up her sleeve. Time to get the nursery sorted, to laze around and enjoy the remaining few weeks of *'selfish, no children life'*. This afternoon she was supposed to be the guest of honour at her baby shower, at the pub in Dingo Beach. She moaned loudly, the niggling back pains that had started twinging innocently this morning had developed into full-blown contractions, the pressure between her legs building until she felt like the baby's head had thrust out from where it should be nestled up, sound asleep, awaiting an 'on the due date' arrival into life.

The car rattled over the dirt track as Simon sped up, driving like a madman and attempting to call the ambulance on his mobile phone as he went. He yelled at the phone before tossing it on the passenger's seat. Taking a quick glimpse back at her he told her the obvious, that there was no mobile reception where they were. They were in a black hole.

He was trying to sound official and in control, but, she closed her eyes, he wasn't fooling her. His voice was panicky, the words tumbling out quicker than usual. Simon didn't usually move fast. He had that laid-back, slow talk and walk, that seemed to be part of living in the north. Thank goodness he'd only been in a nearby paddock fixing fences when she'd rung to tell him her contractions had started and they were coming hard and fast. He'd rushed home, guiding her to the car as he tried to persuade her to sit in the front seat. That had not been an option. There was no way she could sit, the pain so severe that she'd hardly been able to put one foot in front of the other. She'd bent over the bonnet for a few minutes —or one contraction worth— before she'd clambered into the back seat, lowering her body slowly onto the seat and wishing the pain would stop.

Simon had helped her lie down, an old towel he placed under her head as a pillow now held tight in her hands, scrunched up and pressed against her face. Maybe if she blocked out the light, it would all go away. The doctor had said that she might get contractions that would come and go, and then eventually stop. False alarms, or Braxton Hicks he'd called them. 'Don't come in until you really need to. You don't want to be hanging around the wards if you could be at home.' He'd smiled at her in a condescending way. 'First-time mothers often panic with the tiny hint of even a twinge of pain. There's plenty of time. Now, remember, no need to come in until you absolutely have to.'

Great advice, Frankie thought. Let's just all be cool, calm and collected and this baby will just glide out when it's supposed to. Have your bags packed just in case, they'd told her and Simon. Who had time to grab a bag or check the hospital list for what to bring, when shooting pains wracked your body and your stomach was so hard and tight that you couldn't even walk to the car, or bend your body enough to sit down? She bit her lip. They needed time. The hospital was an hour away and they wouldn't get mobile reception for another fifteen minutes or so. By then it would be quicker to drive themselves. Simon would get her there before the ambulance was anywhere nearby.

He turned around to look at her again, this time speaking slowly as if she was a child. 'How are you going? Are they going away?'

Another contraction tightened her muscles, ripping

3

through her body like a tsunami. She thought, at that moment, how much she hated him. Loathed him. This was his fault. She hadn't planned on a pregnancy. It wasn't on her list of, 'to do'. Just because she'd slipped up and forgotten her pill for a couple of nights. Who knew she'd be punished for being forgetful? She'd been busy with her job and thought it wouldn't make a difference. Years ago she had missed taking the pill and nothing had happened. Even though she was now thirty-five, she'd only been with Simon for a couple of years. Besides, he had his own grown-up children and she wasn't even sure she wanted to have babies. She shrieked as a stabbing pain pushed down between her legs, her back arching as she braced and pressed her hands into the back of the driver's seat.

Her words came out between low moans, her stomach clenching tighter, the agony increasing. 'Slow down. No bumps. The pain. I can't take it anymore.'

Simon slowed the car to a crawl. Every pothole or bump the car went over was like a knife driving into her body. She wanted him to stop. To stop the car and to stop the pain. He needed to fix the dilemma, to solve the problem like he always did. Now when he spoke it sounded like he wasn't even trying to mask his panic, his voice frantic. 'I can't stop. We'll never get there if I go any slower. I'm sorry but we have to keep driving. I don't think the contractions are going to go away.'

She pushed herself up onto her knees, her face pushed into the towel as she rocked back and forth. 'The pain is so bad. You need to make it stop.'

'It won't go away just because I stop driving. I need to get you to the hospital. We don't want to be stuck here!' He grabbed the phone again, tapping the numbers aggressively, swearing loudly when the call wouldn't go through. 'There's no reception along this way. There never has been.'

Her voice was a whisper. 'I think my water just broke.'

He turned his head to look at her. 'Shit!'

She curled back into a ball, lying on her side, aware the seat under her was now wet. Breathing in deeply she relished the few seconds without pain. Her eyes remained closed even when Simon stopped the car and jumped out, yelling out to a vehicle coming from the other direction. 'It's Rose's mum, Cecily,' he called to Frankie.

'The eggs,' Frankie muttered back. 'She's delivering eggs and honey for me.'

'Maybe her phone will have reception here. She can ring the ambulance for us,' Simon shouted.

Frankie tried to sit up, but as soon as she moved, another contraction tightened across her torso. She moaned and tried to shuffle her body upright but the pain was crippling and she yelled for Simon. Through her agony she saw Cecily open the back door, her concerned face peering down at her.

Cecily's voice was calm. 'You're in a bad way, my love. How far apart do you think they are?'

Frankie closed her eyes, unable to speak, nodding as Simon answered for her. 'They're about two to three minutes apart and they've been like that for the past hour. Frankie rang me, I was out in the paddock and we hopped straight in the car. I can't get reception on this.' He shook his phone high in the air as if that was going to make it work. 'Can you ring the ambulance? We need to get her to the hospital.'

Cecily passed her phone to Simon. 'You ring. Mine

should get reception here.' She climbed in beside Frankie, holding her hand and giving it a quick squeeze, before running her hands over Frankie's tight belly.

'How many weeks are you?'

'Thirty-six.'

Cecily seemed to be calculating the situation.

Frankie gritted her teeth. 'I need to push. I have to push.'

Simon put his head in through the doorway. 'No pushing. You're not allowed to push. Listen to me, Frankie, no pushing. Listen to my instructions, just breathe in. The ambulance is on its way. Cecily's phone worked here and I'm talking to them now.'

Frankie glared at Simon, her words coming out between ragged breaths. 'Don't tell me not to push. I need to. This is all your fault.'

Simon's eyes were wide and he went to speak but Cecily hushed him. 'Simon, you keep on the line to the ambos and tell them that Frankie's going to start pushing. We'll follow any instructions but also tell them that I'm here, and I've delivered babies before. I was a midwife up in the Territory. You make sure you tell them the baby's coming.'

Cecily turned back to Frankie. 'I'm going to help you sit up and we'll rest your back on the car door. That way you can get your legs up and feel more comfortable. You can't deal with those contractions flat on your back and if you need to push that will work better. We need those knickers off also, love, they'll get in the way.'

Waves of panic rolled over her and she reached for Simon's hand as he sat in the passenger's seat talking to the ambulance who were now on their way.

His eyes were wide, his words tumbling out. 'You'll be okay. Cecily is here and she knows what to do. We're both here for you and the ambulance will be here shortly.'

Frankie wriggled backward and with Cecily's help manoeuvred herself so that her back was upright. Panic gripped her and she tried to follow Cecily's instructions to breathe. She grasped her leg on one side, clutching the front seat with her other hand, as the urge to press down overwhelmed her. Thankfully Cecily pushed back on her knees, at least giving her something to leverage on.

The pain intensified and intense pressure built between her legs. Cecily's voice was calm as she instructed Simon to squat down beside Frankie in the small space beside her. Cecily positioned herself between Frankie's legs as Frankie gripped Simon's arm, her screams reverberating around the car with each contraction.

In between contractions, Simon wiped her face. 'You can do it. I'm here with you. You're doing amazing and the ambulance will come quickly.'

Tears streamed down her face and Simon wiped them away with a tissue. She could barely talk. 'The pain is so bad,' she said. 'The pressure. The pressure is down there.' She noticed the concerned looks passing between Cecily and Simon.

Cecily pushed Frankie's hair back from her face, beads of sweat on her forehead as she felt Frankie's stomach again. 'Simon, wipe my brow with that tissue.' She waited. 'I want you to move behind Frankie and position yourself. Prop her up and let her push back onto you.'

She waited until he was in position, Frankie moaning

as he moved her forward so that he could get in behind her.

Cecily continued. 'Now listen carefully, Frankie. I want you to push really hard with this next one. Push down into your bottom.'

The words were barely out when the next urge rippled through her body. She gripped her knees and pushed as hard as she could. Minutes passed and her energy waned. Exhaustion heaved in every part of her body and her breath came out in noisy gasps. She thought she was fit but this was at an entirely different level than her regular exercise.

Cecily inched forward a bit, her hands moving between Frankie's legs.

She worked as she talked. 'The head is here, Frankie. Now listen carefully and you must do as I say. I want you to pant, don't push, right now, don't push.'

When the urge to push bore down, Frankie resisted, using all her muscles to clench backward, her chest heaving, her back pushed back against Simon's chest. Cecily kept talking to her, her voice the only sane thing in between the pain, the steady instructions giving her something to focus on.

She could feel Cecily between her legs, her hands moving and manoeuvring whatever it was down there. Taking deep breaths she clenched her eyes shut, terrified as she waited for the next urge to push. 'I'm not sure I can do that again. Another one will come.'

'Simon wiped her brow. 'It's okay. Listen to Cecily. You're going to be okay.'

Cecily leaned over her, glancing at Simon, before once again speaking sternly to her. Frankie listened, her eyes opening and focussing on Cecily's. 'You've done great. I've fixed what I needed to. No more holding back now. When the next push comes I want you to give it everything you have. Use all your muscles and every bit of energy you have and push down towards your bottom again. One good push and I reckon you can get this little one out. You're doing great and you're nearly there.'

Simon held her hand tight, his body supporting her when she leaned back on him. Thank God he was here with her. She'd never been so scared in her life. 'I want the pain to go,' she said between clenched teeth.

'It will,' Cecily said. 'It will. Your stomach is tightening. Push, Frankie. Push. Give it everything.'

Simon helped her sit up as much as she could, both her hands clutching her knees. 'Look at me,' Cecily said, 'look straight at me and get that baby out.'

Frankie clenched her muscles, an overwhelming urge wracking her body. Her entire stomach moved and suddenly she felt a release of pressure. The heaviness that had pressed down between her legs eased and the contractions diminished, her stomach no longer tight and gripping. Her energy was spent and she gasped for air as she sprawled back against Simon. His arms held her tight. 'Don't let go of me,' she whispered, feeling his chin on the top of her head.

His words were barely audible. 'Open your eyes. Open your eyes, Frankie.'

Her chest heaved and she took a couple of deep breaths, the absence of contracting pain in her stomach the best release in the world. She peered down at Cecily who crouched between her legs as she held up a squirming bundle of wrinkly arms and legs, the umbilical cord still attached, thick, and bloodied.

Cecily held a baby in her hands, a broad smile crossing her face as she looked at Frankie and Simon. Red lights flashed outside the car and two paramedics peered in through the front windows, just as Cecily announced, 'It's a girl.'

CHAPTER 2

*I*t was two years since Frankie had fallen in love with Simon and made the decision to leave behind her old life on the Gold Coast and stay at Dingo Beach. They hadn't known each other that long when he'd asked her to move into his home and make a new life with him in the Whitsunday region in North Queensland.

At the time the decision had been easy, although she never would have believed anything like it would happen when she'd arrived for a work contract that was only supposed to last a month. The last thing she had been looking for was a romance. It had been a whirlwind spin, although the first time they met, Frankie had not been impressed with Simon or his tractor that had caused her to run off the road and into a muddy ditch. The fact that the road wasn't actually a road but rather a track through Simon's farm was beside the point. After a series of events that had pushed them together, she had fallen for his charms, tumbled head over heels in love, and wanted to be with him every waking minute.

Simon had also been besotted and wooed her with fresh fish and mud crab, a heavenly setting on the beach, and romantic dates.

They were kindred spirits, best friends, and lovers. He was everything she'd ever wanted in a man and for the first year, she felt like she was on a long honeymoon. Not that they'd talked about marriage, they were both happy the way it was. Simon had been married before and his eldest son, Eli, lived in Frankie's apartment on the Gold Coast. Eli's girlfriend Rose lived with him, and they were both in their second year of study at university. The only other family Simon had was a daughter, Amelia, who lived in Cairns with her mother and only seemed to ring him when she was after money or had argued with his ex-wife, Yvette.

Not only had Frankie taken on a new partner and place to live but she'd also tossed in her old job and found herself a new one. Right from the start, her new role with the council turtle breeding program suited her skills and fulfilled the change she was looking for. It was a long time since she had been so passionate about work and instead of trying to please the boss, or climb the ladder to higher positions, now she was part of a team. A group of like-minded people who valued her input and worked together to get the best outcome for the turtle breeding grounds in the Whitsundays. She'd found her niche and living with Simon completed her life in a way she had not dreamed was possible. When her parents visited at different times with their respective partners and approved of her decision, even showing excitement with her new life, her world was complete. For once she had made a good choice.

Life was cruisy, her job only a short drive away and the weekends were filled with fishing and relaxing on the beach. Long walks through the surrounding hills with Simon and short boat trips out to the nearby islands developed her love for the pristine area even more and the fact that Simon wined and dined her continually and spoilt her with an abundance of fresh seafood and beautiful meals, ensured she settled in and wanted to stay. Living together in his old farmhouse in amongst the cane fields, with the ocean and their own private beach as their backyard was the ultimate and her old life was a distant memory.

Simon had admitted that he'd been worried about how a city girl would cope with life where he lived. It was an isolated spot and in summer there was persistent humidity and searing high temperatures, along with midges and other annoying insects that came in every shape and size. In summer, cyclones travelled up and down the coastline, their strong winds and torrential rain a consistent threat during the wet season. She'd felt a taste of the power of one last year when it edged close to where they lived, before veering away. That's what they did, Simon had told her. Unpredictable. He'd warned her that the wind and rain she'd experienced from that last one was nothing. 'More like a storm than a cyclone,' he'd said. 'It's the big ones we worry about, not those little ones. We're in prime position here and often they swing in and head straight across the coastline. If you're here during one of those you'll know about it.'

She'd found the seasons different from where she came from on the Gold Coast. The summers were so hot and humid that she'd needed to spend much of the day inside in the air conditioning. Even hanging the clothes out posed a risk of sunburn and she'd learned to structure her day around the cooler hours of the morning and evening, leaving the middle of the day for inside activities. When winter came it reminded her of mild summers down south and she packed away her jumpers and coats, only the occasional cool night or morning requiring anything other than summer clothes.

She had been living with Simon for a year and a half when she'd fallen pregnant. Right from the start of their relationship they'd discussed that she was on the pill and was not keen to take any risks of having a baby. At that time, Simon had a seventeen-year-old son and thirteen-year-old daughter and he felt like he'd done his share of raising kids. He'd made sure they'd talked about what they wanted regarding a family. He didn't want to have more children, but he'd respect her wishes and they could discuss it if it was something she really wanted. She'd breathed a sigh of relief at the time. Having babies was not something she'd thought about and she was happy with just her and Simon as a family. Maybe she'd get a dog later if she wanted, but life was great the way it was with just the two of them. Thank goodness they were on the same page when it came to the subject of having children.

At Easter time she'd thought her tiredness was from the long hours she'd been working and time spent in the garden. The last few months had been full-on and the two weeks she'd taken off were a welcome break. Obviously, her body needed to rest because all she wanted to do was sleep. An overload of chocolate eggs that Simon spoiled her with was most likely the cause of feeling ill and the squirming unsettled feeling in her stomach would go once the rich food and the over-eating of anything she could lay her hands on, passed.

It was strange that she didn't feel like alcohol or coffee and she wondered if she should go to the doctor and get a check-up. Something didn't feel right and at work a few times she had needed to sit down, dizzy spells causing her to pause and gather herself before continuing with whatever it was she was doing. That was the other problem. Her memory was playing up and as much as she tried to hide it, a couple of work friends had commented that she was a bit absent-minded and had even forgotten important meetings that she had organised.

At the time one of them had joked. 'You're not pregnant, are you? You remind me of my wife when she was expecting our first.'

She'd laughed it off. 'At least I know it's not that. Simon and I agreed about not having kids. He has two and I'm going to get a pup in a couple of months. We're more than happy with it just being the two of us.'

She'd missed her last two periods but that was nothing unusual. She was never regular anyway. The crunch had come when Simon had served her favourite dish. Crab, and more crab.

They'd sat on the beach, near the water, the warmth of the day still heating the sand as the cool of the May night air started to filter in. She loved this time of year. No midges or mossies and in the last couple of weeks she'd even regularly swam, without the worry of stingers.

Her new home was paradise and she wrapped her arms around Simon and kissed him, their eyes meeting as he pulled her in towards him. 'I love it here,' she said, pulling back a bit, her breasts tender as they pushed into his chest.

'If it wasn't for this crab waiting to be eaten, I'd carry you back up to the house and have a repeat of this morning,' Simon said as he smiled at her, his hands rubbing softly up and down her arms. Ripples of excitement ran through her body as his blue eyes locked on hers and she gazed at his rugged face. It was hard not to love Simon. He spoiled her rotten and one of his greatest delights was putting out a seafood spread that he knew she loved.

He pulled out a chair for her as she stared at the crab, displayed beautifully on a large silver plate. Sauces in small dishes encircled the larger plate and Simon leaned over and started serving salad from another bowl. His arms were tanned and strong from working on the farm and his body fit and muscly. A tingly sensation fluttered in her stomach and she tried to stop thinking about this morning. Another luxury was that they had an entire house to themselves, with no one to worry about what time they got out of bed. She took a deep breath just before he leaned over and kissed her. When he pulled away from her she closed her eyes and soaked in the moment. It was the way he looked at her, a look of love but also desire. Perhaps she should let him carry her back up to the house.

She opened her eyes and breathed in deeply, staring out across the ocean. Sparkling diamonds on the surface glimmered in the afternoon sun and the blue of the sky darkened, the palm trees laden with coconuts swaying gently in the afternoon breeze. A row of seagulls perched on the timber jetty Simon had built for her, a couple of them taking off to pursue a ball of bait fish that flickered in the ocean not far in front.

A dizzy feeling spun in her head and she concentrated on the beach, trying to focus on the tranquil scene as she watched a small boat skip across the surface. She watched it until it cleared the nearby headland. When she placed her hands on her stomach to try and stop the rolling feeling in her body a look of apprehension crossed Simon's face.

'Are you okay,' he asked, his eyes wide with concern. 'You've gone pale.'

'I feel like I'm seasick. One minute I was thinking how I'd love you to carry me back upstairs and the next minute my head is spinning. I'll be fine, maybe I just need to eat.'

His eyes narrowed. 'You've been feeling sick a lot lately, plus you're always tired.'

She straightened up and smiled at him. 'Don't worry. I'm okay. I'd just been busy at work, that's all.'

'Maybe you should go for a check-up. You've been talking about it for a while. I can book you in with my doctor.'

'I'm okay.'

He reached over and broke the crab apart, offering her the largest claw.

She stared hard at it, the bile rising in her throat. 'I'm not hungry. I don't think I want it.'

When he placed the claw back in the bowl his eyes turned back to her. 'That's the first time I've ever seen you refuse crab.' He sat upright, his mouth twisted in a way that showed he was thinking hard.

Her stomach churned and she leaned back in her chair, trying to stop the dizziness and nausea.

Simon's eyes met hers. 'When was the last time you had your period?'

'God, you sound like a doctor. It's been a few months but that's not uncommon for me. You know they're all over the place.'

'Are you still on the pill?'

'Of course, I am. What sort of question is that?'

He passed her a glass of water, his eyes wide as he reached over and held her hand. He twisted his fingers through hers, before pushing a strand of hair back from her face. Even though her hair was long she rarely wore it out these days. It was too hot and although once she'd straightened it every morning, now she left it curly and tied up in a ponytail. Pulling the hair band out she twirled the long strands of brown hair around her fingers and coiled it on top of her head. Simon followed her movements, his eyes narrowing when she leaned back and shut her eyes.

'Seriously Simon, I'm fine. Just a bit off-color. I feel a bit better now my hair's up. It was hot on my neck.'

When she opened her eyes he was still staring at her.

'How about we drive to the medical centre?' he said.

'What for?'

'I hate to break it to you Frankie, but I'd take a good bet on it that you're pregnant.' He held up his hand to stop her talking. 'I know you're on the pill, but a couple of times you admitted that you'd taken it the next morning instead of the night before. Think about it, you're sick, late with your periods, and,' he passed his hand gently over her breasts. 'These are definitely larger than normal.'

She shook her head and sat upright. 'What do you think, just because my breasts grow that I'm pregnant?'

He pushed gently on one. 'Are they tender.'

'Ouch,' she said, grabbing his hand and pulling it away from her body. 'Don't. That hurts!'

CHAPTER 3

he next night they sat on the end of the jetty, their hands joined as they stared out across the ocean. Stars flickered brightly, the moon hidden behind the hills, its golden glow invisible from where they sat. Darkness cloaked the water and the sound of the lapping waves was the only noise to be heard.

A scent from a magnolia bush wafted across to where they sat and Frankie inhaled, the sweet smell, pleasant to her senses. In twenty-four hours, her life had been turned on its head. A pregnancy, a baby due in December. Her body was changing already and soon it would be unrecognisable. Ahead of her, a life of dirty nappies, screaming noises and broken sleep. Simon had not reacted how she had thought he would. He wasn't worried at all. In fact he was excited, happy, one might even say euphoric and hadn't stopped hugging her every opportunity he got. She'd had to ask him to stop staring at her like she was fragile or asking her if she needed anything. He was positively beaming. On the other hand, she hadn't smiled once since the doctor said those words. 'Yes dear, you are pregnant. No dear, I don't make mistakes. I'd say you're about two months but the scans you'll need to organise will give you the exact date. Make sure you book in for that and also with the hospital. Christmas is a busy time to have a baby.'

When she'd asked how this could have happened, both the doctor and Simon had laughed. Their deep chuckles weren't what she needed to hear. She needed sympathy, people to console her, and agree that this was a terrible predicament to be in and that perhaps the doctor had made a mistake.

Perhaps her father would offer sympathy. He'd understand that this hadn't been in her plans, she'd never had anything to do with babies, and of all people he would appreciate how this would upset her career prospects with her new job. She babbled out the news when she rang him, rushing her words, re-iterating every negative aspect of her dilemma.

His response shocked her. He was ecstatic. Thank goodness she hadn't waited any longer because he was in his sixties now and well overdue for a grandchild. It was just as well because she was getting older so this was perfect. His excitement had resonated in her ears. There would be time for him to come and see her, she'd make a wonderful mother, and what a perfect age for childbearing. He wanted to know if it would be alright if he and Peggy—his wife—bought the cot and pram. Were they going to find out what sex it was? When was a good time to visit and did she need any help with anything else in the meantime?

She'd hung up feeling deflated. It had not been what

21

she'd expected and she took deep breaths, consoling herself that her father had aged, he was not thinking rationally and had probably forgotten what bringing up a baby was really like. Her mother, Kate, would understand and be more empathetic and compassionate.

Her mother had been even more excited than her father. 'It's high time, Frankie. That biological clock of yours is ticking fast. If I was you, I wouldn't leave it too long before you go for number two. Don't wait years between this baby, and the next ones. Make sure you have that second one as soon as you can. This is just the best news ever. I need to be called Nana and once the weather cools down up there I'll come and stay. You know, give you a hand. I'll start putting a pack of baby things together for you.'

Heaven forbid, what was her mother even thinking, suggesting a second one. She couldn't even get her head around one. She glanced at Simon who was staring at her.

Laughing loudly, he leaned over to kiss her. 'It's okay. We'll be fine.'

She glared at him. 'What's so funny? This isn't a laughing matter. You're not the one with an alien thing growing inside of you and hormones bouncing in every direction. My head is all over the place and my body no longer feels like it belongs to me.'

His look softened and he stroked her arm. 'You're due just before Christmas. It will be the middle of summer and stinking hot. I'll get a new air-con put in that spare room and do it up. You tell me what colour you want it painted and we can buy some new furniture for in there. That can be the baby's room.

She stretched her legs out in front of her. While she

had been thinking about what was in store for her and her body and what she was going to say at work, Simon had been dreaming about the baby's room and how to keep it cool. 'You almost sound like this is something to look forward to.'

He grinned broadly. 'I've had time to sleep on it. It's pretty bloody exciting. I never thought I'd have any more kids. He squeezed her hand. 'What do you hope it will be? A boy or girl. It'll be great to have another little fella running around. Look at Eli, he's never been much trouble. On the other hand, I've hardly had anything to do with Amelia after her mother took her away. It would be nice to have a little girl. One I can watch grow up. Take care of ...'

Frankie cut him off. 'I can't believe that you think this is a good thing for us. I can't think past tonight. There's something in my stomach growing and in seven months it will be here and my life will never be the same again.' Her voice shook and tears welled in her eyes. That was the other annoying issue lately. She cried at the drop of a hat. She'd always been proud of the fact that she wasn't emotional or sooky. The saddest movie in the world could be playing yet she'd be the one handing out tissues to her girlfriends as they sobbed and wailed over romantic sagas, yet not a tear in her eye. When things got tough, she put her chin out and became determined and resolute. Steadfast, unemotional, and unruffled.

'I don't...' she took a deep breath trying to compose herself and keep her voice level. 'I don't care.' With that she burst into tears, throwing herself into Simon's arms. He held her tight, stroking her back and wiping her face. 'I don't care what it is,' she said through her sobs. 'I just want my body back. I don't want a baby. I don't even know how to look after one. I've never even changed a nappy.'

She was sure she saw the hint of a smile on his face as he straightened up and pushed her hair back from her face. It looked like he was trying to appear serious. Anger welled inside of her and she felt her face redden. 'Why is it always up to the woman to look after the contraception side of life? Why didn't you have some responsibility in stopping me from falling pregnant?'

She glared at him, noticing he was going to unusual lengths to keep his voice calm, that condoling expression on his face she knew was a put-on. 'I would have, except you assured me several times that you had it all under control.' He pulled her in tight again. 'You'll be okay. We're in this together. It's not as if you're fifteen and there's no one to look after you.' He chuckled, rankling her further. 'It's just, instead of two, we will be three.'

A retort swirled in her mind, but the words didn't come quick enough and warm lips pressed down on hers. 'I know what will make you feel better,' he whispered in her ear.

She kissed him back. 'That's what got us into this bother to begin with.'

'So, is that a, no?'

She stood up as he pulled her to her feet, his arms wrapping around her, his kisses sweet. She tried not to smile, shaking her head as he held her at arm's length. 'You're just too charming. That's the problem,' she said.

'You should see how beautiful you look.' He stroked her face and grabbed her hand. 'Come with me my beautiful Frankie, and I'll make you forget about everything.'

This time she laughed, hanging onto his arm as they walked up the path toward the house.

* * *

That week Simon had surprised her with a delicious meal down on the beach. As she ate she listened to him talk about his plans for the farm. Thank goodness she was starting to feel a bit better and could once again eat seafood. Her appetite had gone from one extreme to the other and now she was constantly hungry. She watched as he stood up and came towards her. When he looked at her and she thought he was going to make a joke about how much she had eaten. It was a wonder she hadn't scared him off. She'd been so cranky lately and kept telling him she wanted her body back the way it should be. Thank goodness he understood her moods and why she was acting the way she was.

She scowled at him, unsure what he was up to as he moved towards her. 'What?' she said. 'What are you going to tell me?'

It took a moment for his actions to sink in. He crouched in front of her then knelt on one knee, his hand reaching into his pocket before pulling out a ring. A solitary diamond on a gold band sparkled as the sun hit it.

She gasped out loud, his next words taking her completely by surprise. 'Frankie. I thought this was the best place to ask you. We've had so many happy times here. Will you be my wife, marry me and be with me forever?'

Laughter and tears came all at once when he slipped

the beautiful ring on her finger. 'Oh, my goodness. Yes, of course, I will marry you.'

They'd lay together on the sun lounge, the shade of the trees providing a cool spot, the ocean in front a romantic setting as they talked about the years ahead. 'We can get married before the baby or after it comes. It's up to you, whatever you want,' he whispered in her ear.

Her hand waved in front of them and he laughed as she tilted the ring one way and then the other. 'I can't believe it. We're engaged,' she said. 'I don't think I'll have the energy to worry about a wedding now. Let's leave it until after the baby is born. She placed her hands on her stomach and he wrapped his over the top of hers. 'This is what makes me happy,' she told him. 'You and me. It's like the world outside has stopped and it's just about us.'

'I love you, Frankie,' he said, hugging her as she nestled into his shoulder.

'I love you more,' she replied.

CHAPTER 4

The metal Hills hoist spun with the breeze. The wind had blown for weeks and gritty dust settled on everything, inside and outside the house. Frankie struggled with the sheets, the fabric twisting and flapping, making it impossible to hang them out neatly, the way she wanted. The dogs, Demi and Macee, yapped at her feet, jumping up and trying to bite her towels that swung wildly on the clothesline. She yelled at them to be quiet, but her words were lost in the wind and the dogs chased each other, a new yellow towel plucked from the clothesline firmly in Macee's mouth, its length draping across the dirt.

Macee rolled on the ground, the towel twisted in amongst her legs. She was what Simon called a bitsa dog, a bit of this and a bit of that. Her large body with black spots on white fur, led them to believe that perhaps the dalmatian from the farm next door may have some connection to her. Simon had got her and the smaller dog, Demi, from farms not too far away when they were pups, so it was possible the neighbourhood dogs were all related.

Frankie walked slowly towards Macee, but Demi blocked her path, yapping and jumping up, her dirty paws leaving their mark on Frankie's white skirt.

She had asked Simon to do something about the ground under the clothesline, to plant some grass or pave it so that she didn't have to contend with the dirt when it was dry. He'd said he would, but he'd been too busy with the farm as well as painting inside the house.

When Frankie stepped around the smaller dog and went to rescue her towel, Macee thought that she was playing a game of tag. The spotted dog took off in leaps and bounds, stopping when Frankie got near her but then running off again when her hand reached out to get her towel. Both dogs ran in circles, jumping over the washing basket that held all the clean wet clothes, ready to be hung out. They raced in and out of the bushes at the side of the house, cavorting wildly and at one stage both on either end of the towel as they played a game of tug of war. In the end Frankie gave up and sat down on an over-turned bucket, waiting until they came to her. They didn't though. They sat at arm's distance, tongues hanging out, panting as they waited for her to get up and chase them.

The dogs were Simon's and as much as she tried to discipline them, they took no notice of her. They loved her, that was clear, but they wouldn't follow her instructions or come when they were called. They clearly considered her a newbie and when Simon wasn't around, they played merry hell with whatever she wanted them to do. Of course, when Simon was there, they were perfect, butter wouldn't melt in their mouths. She glared at them as they stared back at her.

Just as she was about to get up and chase them again, Demi growled. Both dogs sat up, their ears pricked forward. Frankie turned around, groaning loudly as she watched a ute drive in through the gate. It belonged to the farmer whose property adjoined Simon's. The farmer's name was Artie and he had been a thorn in her side the last couple of weeks. She'd never really had much to do with him until lately. Before now she had been at work most days, however recently her boss, Ken, had asked if she'd like to cut back to three days a week. An over-whelming lethargy and nausea came and went, at no particular time and for no reason. Ken didn't mind if she reduced her hours and once she had the baby she could come back full-time, whenever she was ready.

She'd discussed the matter with Simon and as much as she hated the idea of not working she had given in. Her energy levels were all over the place and it didn't matter what vitamins she took or what advice she followed, her body was tired and she constantly wanted to sleep. Her blood pressure and iron levels were low and the doctor had instructed that she take it easy. 'We don't want complications for you or the baby,' he'd said.

So, she relented and every Thursday and Friday she stayed at home. She had to admit she was enjoying the relaxation, and time to catch up on sleep and other chores that she'd pushed to the side. There was even time to read some novels, books that she'd had her eye on for years and hadn't had time to pick up.

The trouble was, every time she sat down in her favourite spot overlooking the beach, something would disturb her. Last week it had been Artie's horses. His fences needed fixing and his seven, very unfriendly horses, had pushed their way through the flimsy wire and came close to where she sat. They picked at the lush green grass that grew under the shade of the sprawling trees. Simon assured her that they'd been coming over to his place for years, picking at the green shoots of grass that were plentiful in the cooler spots. Frankie didn't really care if the tradition was years old, the horses were ruining her quiet days at home. Apart from the fact that they blocked her path back up to the house, they also stirred the dogs into a continuous roll of frenzied barking.

If she tried to shoo the horses away or walk near them, they swung their heads, flattened their ears, and bucked and jumped at a dangerously close proximity. One day she'd had to ring Simon because she'd been stuck on the jetty for over an hour. Every time she moved, they came towards her, the dogs stirring them up even more when they barked and nipped at the horse's legs.

Simon, who had been out on his tractor somewhere amidst the cane, had calmed her down and then rung Artie. Artie had eventually wandered over, appearing through the bushes, a wide grin on his face.

Frankie guessed that Artie was about seventy-five, his belly showing the signs of living a contented life, probably full of beer and crab just like every other Dingo Beach local. Every time she'd seen him, he wore the same clothes. Navy blue King Gee shorts and a khaki green work shirt, a tattered Akubra hat pushed down on his head. His legs reminded her of a football player's. Solid and stocky, with bulging calf muscles, his bare feet stomping across the ground, slowly and methodically.

What was it with people in North Queensland, she thought, they never rushed, smiled when there was nothing to smile about and rarely stressed about tricky situations. Situations like her being on the jetty, in the hot sun when perhaps she needed to go to the toilet or have something to eat. Maybe it would be nice if she was able to walk safely through her own backyard without the threat of a mob of horses accosting her.

Eying him warily she watched as he raised his hand and called out, 'G'day Frankie. How you going, love?' She'd never seen him wear shoes. Always barefoot, his hardened feet tramping on thistles and those deadly three-cornered prickles that always seemed to find a way through her thinly soled shoes. Not Artie's feet though, they must be as tough as nails.

Over the last few weeks, she'd had quite a few chats with him. Well, actually she'd complained to him on several occasions. His rubbish tip was near their fence line, and he loved nothing more than to burn rubbish right at the same time as when she hung her washing out. The smoke billowed across their yard, in through her open windows and filtered through the rooms, its smell infiltrating her curtains, lounges and even into her walk-in robe which held her prized dresses and shoes.

'God only knows what he burns,' Simon had said, laughing when she'd complained. 'You won't change Artie's ways. He's been on that farm for generations. Him and Maureen. You just have to get to know him, Frankie. He's a great bloke.'

She'd rolled her eyes. 'That great bloke should also be reported for his cruelty to animals. The other day I drove over to take back a couple of the pups that had wandered over. It's one of his daughter's dogs that's had the pups. She's gone on holiday and he's supposed to be looking after them. They've all been sold so they won't be there for long. He doesn't even keep them locked up. They would have died if I hadn't shown them the way back home.'

'That doesn't make him cruel. Artie loves his animals. Those pups would have wandered back. They're farm animals, it's a bit different than how you have dogs in the city.'

'He greeted me like he was the happiest man on the earth. No concern for the fact that people who had bought the pups were coming to collect them that week and they could have wandered off never to be found again.'

Simon laughed again. 'Artie will never die of stress, I can tell you that.'

She'd pursed her lips and sat up tall. 'It's not a laughing matter, Simon. He does more than just neglect his dogs and horses.'

'Okay, tell me. What did he do?'

'The other day I drove through the back track, right through the cane. I was on my way to yoga at Hideaway Bay. I caught him red-handed.'

'Caught him doing what?' Now she had Simon's full attention.

'He'd run over one of Maureen's cats. He said it came out of the cane and went straight under the tractor tyre. *Flattened it like a piece of paper*, were his words, spoken as always with a smile on his face.'

'Jees, Maureen won't be happy with him. He'll be in trouble over that one.'

'Maureen probably has no idea, because I caught him disposing of it. Hiding the evidence. I came up behind him right when he was getting rid of it.'

'He's a bit deaf. He probably didn't hear your car coming. Was he digging a hole? Knowing Artie he wouldn't want to upset Maureen so he probably got rid of it so she didn't see it. He's very thoughtful.'

'No, he didn't do the humane thing like dig a hole or take it home for Maureen to bury properly. He called it the sugar-cane aerial burial. He held the dead cat by its back legs and twirled it around his head. Like a discus thrower winds up and then lets go.'

Simon grimaced. "I know what you're going to say.'

She pulled a face, showing her disgust. 'He twirled the cat around and around and then flipped it as hard as he could into the cane. It flew like a bird over the top of the flowers, right into the middle of the crop. You would never find it. Can you believe it! *Gone*, he said. *Gone with the wind.*'

Simon laughed. 'The old aerial burial.' He stopped smiling when he looked back at her.

'That's exactly what he called it.'

She could tell Simon was trying to keep a straight face when he replied. 'I mean, it's not that bad. Sometimes it's just too hard to bury them. He's a busy man and he would have made sure it was dead before he threw it. It's not like it suffered.'

'He can't be too busy because he had plenty of time after he'd finished throwing the cat to regale me with several stories about pets that they'd had in the past. One story after the other. I was appalled. It's a wonder the animal welfare isn't onto him.'

Simon had tried to explain to her that pets on farms were different from the pampered ones in the cities and suburbs. 'If a dog's useless sometimes they just shoot it out here on the farms. It's a different way of life.'

She'd been horrified at some of the animal stories she'd heard and the sight of the aerial burial had stayed with her. Barbaric. Inhumane. What sort of people lived in these parts? 'Tell me you have not, or would not ever do that, please.'

Simon's eyes flitted back and forth and she glared at him. 'Please tell me you have never done that.'

'No, of course not. Never.'

She recalled the sight of the cat flying over the cane now, as Artie pulled up in his ute. Both dogs wagged their tails and gave friendly barks once they saw who it was. Artie's dog, Riley, left his position in the passenger's seat, jumping straight out through the open window, the spotted dalmatian leaping and running around with Macee and Demi. Frankie shook her head as they raced around, barking wildly, cavorting, and jumping until they eventually knocked over the washing basket. The contents spilled onto the dust. Riley twisted back, grabbing her new maternity designer jeans, the dog's mouth firmly hanging onto the legs as the other two dogs joined in. Soon they were all having a tug of war with the jeans and it was only because Artie yelled at them that they stopped.

Riley picked the jeans up in his mouth, shaking the dust from them before placing them at Artie's feet. The other two dogs lay in the shade next to the house, exhausted from the wild game of tag and tug. Artie patted Riley, talking to the dog like it was the most obedient and skilful animal in the world. With her jeans held high in his hand, Artie walked towards her. She looked down at the ground. What was the use of saying anything?

Her neighbour's smile was wide as he passed the jeans back to her. 'How you going, love? Looks like these were ripped anyway, lots of holes in them that the dogs didn't do. Maybe you should get that Simon to buy you a new pair. He's got plenty of money.'

She took the jeans, shook the dirt from them and folded them neatly. 'It's the style. They're not holes. They're designer jeans and …' She stopped. What was the use?

Artie laughed and pulled up another overturned bucket next to her. 'I know that. I have five daughters. They've all been through the ripped jeans style.' He passed her a glass bottle. 'Maureen made this for you. Simon said you'd been feeling off.'

She took the bottle. God knows what the concoction was. It wouldn't matter because she'd tip it straight down the sink anyway. She'd heard stories about Maureen's homemade Grappa. 'Thanks, but I can't drink alcohol at the moment.'

He took his hat off and banged it on the side of his leg. 'We heard you were having a baby. It's not alcohol. It's a tea Maureen makes that helped her get through morning sickness. There's nothing bad in it, just some herbs and tea she gets from Italy. She made the special mixture up, especially for you.'

'Thanks.'

He stood up, pushing his hat on his head. 'Maureen said to say sorry about the mess the cows made in your garden last week. One of our grandkids left the gate open.'

Frankie raised her eyebrows. 'Tell her it's fine. I just got Simon to get rid of the garden. It was destroyed.'

He smiled at her as he stood up. He always smiled, she thought, even when she was complaining to him, he still smiled at her. It rankled her and she wondered how someone could be consistently calm and not stressed. He spoke quietly, his words always softly spoken. 'Anyway, let us know if you need anything.'

He whistled Riley, who lay with the other dogs in the shade. The dog came straight away, its tail whipping against Frankie's leg as it nestled its nose into Artie's hand. She stared hard at it. Someone had used a black marker and drawn a pair of glasses around its eyes. On its back, other black lines joined the spots on its coat. Like a join-the-dots, puzzle. She screwed up her face, peering curiously at the patterns and marks on the fat dog's body and face.

Artie patted the dog's back. 'Riley loves to eat the avocados. He stands under the tree all day. They make him fat.'

Frankie also stood, her body stiff from sitting on the bucket. She laughed out loud as she viewed the other side of the dog, more marks adorning its legs and under its stomach. 'I was more curious about the drawings on him.'

'The kids did that with their permanent marker pens. They have fun with him.' He tipped his hat. 'I'll get going. No complaints for me today?'

She bit her tongue. What was the use? Yesterday one of his horses had paid a visit and eaten the entire patch of herbs that she had planted in an old bathtub. Now as she looked over to where Riley had been lying down she noticed her flattened seedlings that she'd only planted this morning.

'No, no complaints, Artie.'

CHAPTER 5

The next few months flew past. Working three days was perfect, although the tiredness never seemed to leave her. The nausea had eased for a while but then returned and although the books stated that it should disappear around four months, hers seemed to be lingering. One day she got desperate and considered the tea that Maureen had made for her. Artie called in every week with another bottle and up until now she'd tipped it out on her flower garden. The flowers hadn't died so perhaps there was nothing too deadly in it.

This morning, she'd had enough of everything. She was cranky and tired. Sleep had been intermittent and her back ached from sleeping in the same position. Previously she slept on her stomach but that was becoming more and more impossible. Simon had annoyed her with his jovial attitude, even whistling as he made his breakfast and brought her a cup of tea and toast in bed.

Everyone, including Simon, was excited about the baby. Everyone except her. They weren't the ones with aching legs, a bulging stomach, and nausea that she'd definitely had enough of. She stared hard at the bottle of tea. Maureen had listed the ingredients on the side, a mixture of tea and herbs that she'd called, Maureen's Miraculous Mixture. Frankie took a swig from the bottle and then another. It tasted good. Filling a glass, she decided to head for the beach where she could sit and drink it slowly. Who knew, perhaps it might help.

Now was a good time to get out of the house for a while, before it got too hot. Looking at the ocean and beach always made her feel a little better and she especially loved the small jetty Simon had built for her. If she sat on it and the tide was in she could watch the fish below. Sometimes a stingray or turtle floated past or ducked in under the shade of the timbers, chasing a smaller prey. When she perched on the end of the timbers and dangled her legs above the water the cool salty breeze quelled her sickness a little.

This morning was a perfect time to sit and drink Maureen's Miraculous Mixture, relax and enjoy the view. Pushing a wide straw hat on her head, she held her glass of tea and shut the back door behind her. Demi and Macee followed her, stopping when she did, halfway down the path.

The dogs seemed to have calmed a little in the last few weeks. Perhaps they were getting used to her now that she was home more often. She talked to them, watching both as their hackles rose and they barked loudly, standing firm in front of her. What now, she thought, looking down towards the end of the path. A massive black bull with a huge hump on its back stared back at her. It raised its head a little, long floppy ears swaying back and forth as it slowly ambled towards her on its stumpy legs. The dogs barked loudly, Macee backing up and getting under Demi's longer legs. Frankie's stomach lurched and she turned and jogged slowly back up the path, leaving the dogs to block the way. Luckily she hadn't walked too far and she could easily get back to the house.

Once she was back in the safety of the verandah she whistled and called out. The bull swung its head from side to side, its eyes focussed on the dogs that were growling and barking but also keeping their distance.

For once they obeyed her calls, both scampering away from the encroaching bull and following her into the house. The wooden kitchen door slammed behind them, and she looked down at the dogs who stared back, their tails wagging as if it was all a game. She peered through the window, gasping out loud as she watched the bull push over the old wooden washing trolley that she had filled with a variety of potted plants. The trolley was her pride and joy. He'd rescued it from Simon's shed and fixed it up, the pansies and paper daisies meticulously planted in matching terracotta pots, a bright spot of colour in her garden. She yelled as loudly as she could through the open window, as the bull shoved the trolley out of the way and started pushing the pots in every direction. Macee put her paws on the windowsill and watched the ongoing destruction with her while Demi yapped at her feet as if to let her know she understood how she was feeling. The pots lay scattered, the soil and plants broken and squashed under the hooves of the bull.

Slamming the window shut she told the dogs to lie on the mat. She gritted her teeth. Enough was enough. Why should she have to be trapped in her own home?

Not even able to go and sit quietly down on the water-front. She tipped the glass up, the last of Maureen's concoction cool on her throat. Both dogs had taken advantage of being allowed inside and lay down under the kitchen table. It would be better to leave them there for the moment, rather than letting them out. They'd only chase the bull and then there would be more damage.

She picked up her phone. No more ringing Simon. It was time for her to ring Artie direct. He needed to know in no uncertain terms that she was over his bloody horses and cattle, his smouldering rubbish and most of all his huge ugly black bull. She was going to let him have it.

Maureen answered the phone, her calm, friendly manner antagonising Frankie even more. 'Yes, love, oh that's terrible.' Maureen made tutting noises and listened to Frankie without interrupting. Just as well because Frankie had a lot to tell her and she needed to get it off her chest. 'Oh dear,' Maureen said. 'Not to worry though, I'll get onto Artie. He's up in the cane somewhere, but he'll be home soon and he can come and chase Barney back home. Don't worry about it, that bull won't hurt you. He's as placid as a kitten. Artie can tell you all about his breeding background. Worth a fortune he is. They're usually grey or red, but not our Barney.'

What was it with North Queenslanders, Frankie thought. Who cared what colour bulls were and since when did they have names? Didn't the people around here worry about anything! If the bull was worth so much money, why was it roaming the neighbourhood? Frankie was firm in her reply. "I've had enough, Maureen. I can't take any more stray animals, stories about aerial burials, or smoke filling my house and making my clean washing stink.' It was simple. Surely that wasn't too much to ask.

'That Artie, he's a shocker,' Maureen replied with a chuckle. 'Don't you worry, love, I'll get onto him. Mind you he loves his animals. Treats them like royalty. Sometimes though, men just don't understand and have absolutely no idea of what it's like to be pregnant or run a household. All they worry about is their cattle and the price of sugar.' She added, 'and of course their beer in the afternoon.'

Frankie listened to Maureen's chatter, answering with short replies when she'd asked about her pregnancy. Her voice was like Artie's, calm and slow. 'How's that tea working for you,' Maureen asked. 'It worked a treat for me when I was pregnant with all my girls. I hope you've had enough to last you.' She chuckled. 'These people who think morning sickness is just in the morning and only lasts a few months. Well, I can tell you, they don't know what they're talking about. Ask me. That's why I got hold of that family recipe for the tea. Artie said you're always pleased when he gives it to you. He loves his chats with you. Always gives me the rundown on how you are when he comes home. We're lucky to have good neighbours like you and Simon. Now tell me how this pregnancy is going. What time of the day is worst for you nausea?'

Frankie had to think before she answered. She hadn't felt sick since she'd drunk the mixture this morning. Was it just a rare break from the nausea, a coincidence perhaps? Who cared, she thought, something had worked. She talked to Maureen a bit longer, strangely feeling somewhat calmer from explaining how she felt. Maureen actually listened to her complaints, sympathising about how sick she felt and the sleepless nights, getting up and down to go to the toilet all the time. Her replies were genuine, as if she felt sorry for Frankie and understood exactly how she was feeling. She'd agreed that it was a tough time and even worse when it hadn't been planned. The questions she asked were better than what the doctor usually did and it was good to be able to tell someone exactly what was going on with her body and health. Maureen even had some practical hints for small problems that had been worrying her. She understood how Frankie was feeling. At last, someone who understood.

'From what Artie and Simon tell me, you're doing great, love,' Maureen said. 'You'll get there, but make sure you ring if you need anything or if our animals are bothering you. Don't ring that Artie, ring me and I'll get onto him. He'll get a move on once I tell him what needs to be done.'

Frankie hung up after the long conversation, her previous angry mood lightened by talking to the sympathetic Maureen. She headed towards the kitchen, a load lifted from her shoulders and for the first time in a long while she was hungry, and not feeling nauseous.

* * *

The cooler months were a bit kinder to Frankie and Maureen's tea that she drank each morning gave her more get-up-and-go and kept the sickness away. For a while she felt healthy and energetic, although the movements in her stomach were continual and at times her belly felt like a punching bag. 'It just never stops,' she said to Simon one night. 'When I try and roll over it's all on one side and I can't actually move or get back to the position I was in.'

He'd nuzzled into her neck, his kisses tickling her as he caressed her body. 'You're beautiful. You look incredible.'

'You're lying,' she looked straight into his blue eyes. 'I'm as fat as that black Barney bull next door. How is my body ever going to go back to normal?'

Her mind ticked over as Simon fell back asleep. In the paddocks nearby, cows called out and calves taken from their mothers, bellowed back and forth to one another. A curlew sounded its mournful call, another one taking up the same sound from somewhere on the other side of the yard. In the distance the push of the breeze in the trees sounded, the dull roar of the ocean a background noise, as the tide came in and the wind kicked up its waves.

Her new home and surroundings was beautiful, a tropical paradise. She had become used to the isolation, and the occasional chats with Maureen on the phone kept her positive and on track. Once the baby was born, she'd have the required six weeks at home and then she could go back to work. There was a child-minding facility near where she worked. She'd just pop the baby in there and then pick it up in the afternoon. Hopefully, her life would return to normal. She picked up a book someone had given her on what to feed a toddler. She'd have to learn what babies ate. There was no way she was breastfeeding. Plenty of mothers fed babies using a bottle. It said so in the book. It seemed like the easier option. Her own mother hadn't been able to breastfeed and she'd been brought up on bottled milk. She was okay. The next few months needed to pass quickly and then their life could go back to normal. It would be Simon and her, and yes there would be a baby, but that wouldn't change their life much. They wouldn't let it. She loved her new job and home. The baby would just have to fit in with what they did. It would be simple.

* * *

As September rolled into October the weather changed and began to get warmer. The days grew longer and her due date didn't seem that far off. When she finished up at work they'd thrown a small farewell party for her. It had been sad to say goodbye. The groups she worked with had become her friends and she knew she could call on any one of them if there was something she needed. They would do anything for her as she would for them. It was a tight-knit community and it gave her a warm feeling to be part of it.

Now she'd finished at work there was plenty to do at home. The spare room had been done up and a cot and a few other pieces of furniture made it look like a baby's room. Simon had painted the walls and a couple of her friends from work had made new curtains and helped her cover an old chair that was positioned in the corner. Maureen had called over with a beautiful quilt that she had made for the cot and Simon's son Eli had sent a cute teddy bear from him and Rose that sat on the new shelves Simon had built. The hospital paperwork was done, doctor's visits were up to date, and she'd even read up on what to expect when you're expecting. Not too much though. It was a bit overwhelming, and she skimmed over the childbirth part, choosing to read only the bits that explained the strongest pain relief drugs available. She didn't want to know about all that other stuff. The hospital could handle the medical side of the childbirth procedure, that's what they were there for and these days there were plenty of drugs available so the mother didn't have to go through the pain that women had endured years ago. Her mother had no trouble having her and she intended for her childbirth to be the same.

The bottles and sterilizer were ready, the nappies and wraps washed and folded neatly away and a range of tiny outfits washed and ready to go. She'd always been organised and liked life to be structured and orderly. Having a baby was not going to change any of that. Being prepared and in control was what she was good at.

Simon had started to fuss over her more than usual but she'd let him know there was nothing wrong with her. In a couple of months, she'd be back to herself. Yes, her moods swung like an overwound pendulum and the tears flowed with even the slightest hint of criticism or disagreement. He wanted her to take it easy. 'How much easier can I go? I finished work earlier than normal and now I do nothing except a bit of gardening when the yard is bull free.'

By the start of October she noticed her stomach kept tightening, especially at night when she lay still. It was a strange feeling, like a belt being drawn in firm around her body and then released. 'I think they're like small contractions,' she told the doctor. He'd assured her that it was normal, most women experienced them so it was nothing to worry about. Everything was ticking along nicely, the baby's size was good and she should be ready to deliver by the due date.

No one had ever said anything about going into labour early, or contractions coming so fast that she might not be able to get to the hospital in time. That instead of being in a comfortable hospital bed with caring nurses and anaesthetists who readily supplied pain relief, instead she might be lying on her back on a narrow seat in the back of her small car in the middle of a cane field. No one mentioned that Simon would be squished into the back seat and propping her up from behind, that there would be zero sanitary conditions, no softly calm music playing, or clean crips baby wraps to wrap the newborn baby in. The book hadn't said anything about being on an isolated road with a local woman she barely knew, positioned between her legs, ready to catch whatever was pushed out from her body.

She must have missed those pages that told you what to do if you were stuck on a track with no phone reception or a doctor handy. Nobody ever said that babies didn't wait until you were ready for them to come and that they could force their way into the world no matter where you were. And quickly! Those ridiculous predicaments would never happen to her!

CHAPTER 6

Charlotte White was born on the 12th of October and weighed 3.5 kg. Her hair was dark and she had the most beautiful blue eyes Frankie had ever seen.

The paramedics who were both local men had shown Simon how to cut the cord. The whole time they'd kept talking to Frankie while Cecily made sure she was comfortable. 'I'm Heath and this is Peter,' the taller of the two said. 'We've known Simon since we were all kids, so this is pretty special for us.'

Simon held the baby, her tiny little hands and face sticking out from the bright striped towel she was wrapped in. Although Cecily had everything well under control by the time the baby arrived it was reassuring to have Heath and Peter there. They were friendly and calm and right from the moment they arrived had put everyone at ease. They'd praised Cecily, amazed at how she'd managed to cope and how efficiently she'd delivered a baby in the back seat of the car. Heath had written down notes as they listened to her, asking further questions when she went into detail about how the cord had been around the baby's neck and it was only because Frankie had listened carefully to her instructions and worked hard not to push that she had been able to loosen the cord and continue with the delivery.

'Bloody lucky, mate, that Cecily was coming your way,' Heath said. 'What a champ she is, and your wife. You've all done great. Mother and baby seem fine.'

Simon was lost for words and stood gazing down at the tiny bundle in his arms. 'I'm just trying to gather my thoughts and get over the shock that Frankie just gave birth in the cane fields,' he finally said. Peter came over and steered him to the waiting vehicle, its lights still flashing. 'Let's get moving. You're going in the back with your missus and that new bubba. Have a few moments together.'

Once the men settled everyone in, the ambulance started its journey through the cane fields, enroute to the main road and then the highway that would lead them to the hospital. Frankie watched through the back windows of the ambulance. She could see Cecily who held her hand high, waving them off, a broad grin covering her face, almost as if she had enjoyed the experience. They were indebted to her. She'd saved Frankie and baby Charlotte. Frankie gazed down at the bundle she held. A gorgeous little mouth opened and closed and she stroked the tiny face with her finger. Simon looked down at them. 'You're amazing, Frankie. Just amazing.'

'She's so perfect. Just beautiful,' she replied, unable to take her eyes away from the baby's face. 'I love her so much already. She's ours, Simon. Our own baby.'

The shock of what had just happened was starting to

sink in and she closed her eyes, her body and mind exhausted. Thank goodness the pain was gone, the agony that had wracked her body this morning had disappeared. She looked at Simon and then the baby. Charlotte. Now they were a family of three.

* * *

Life after having Charlotte was completely different than she had envisaged. It wouldn't have mattered if anyone had told her what it would be like, she wouldn't have believed them anyway. Just like the baby books said, the days were spent feeding, changing nappies, and washing. But she didn't hate it like she thought she would. It wasn't a chore and her decision to only feed by bottle had gone out the window. Cecily visited her at the hospital the day after the birth and encouraged her to breastfeed if she could, but Frankie had already thought about it, even in the ambulance on the way to the hospital. It was amazing how your ideas changed once you held that little bundle in your arms.

Once she was settled back in at home, the neighbours all called in with presents and flowers. Artie and Maureen checked on her regularly, dropping in to make sure she had everything she needed. She'd become part of the community, around her, a collection of people of all different ages and backgrounds who genuinely cared about her.

Bert, who had been the cleaner at the motel where Frankie had stayed when she first arrived at Dingo Beach, called in with his wife. Myrtle had dementia and Bert held tightly to her arm as he guided her down the pathway to sit under the trees in the cool of the shade.

It was nearly Christmas and heavy clouds clustered on the horizon, their bottoms dark and bruised. A stifling humidity hung heavy, and the grass crackled under their feet as they walked on it. It was dry and hot and the word was that the monsoon rains or perhaps even a cyclone would come soon. Simon pulled out chairs for Myrtle and Frankie, before pouring them all a cool drink. They sat back, relaxing and talking about the events of the previous months. Bert laughed loudly when Simon repeated the story of the birth in the back seat of the car.

'That Cecily is worth her weight in gold,' Bert chuckled. 'I don't know how she manages, her husband has always worked away a lot and she's brought up all those kids virtually by herself. She deserves a bloody medal. Well done Frankie. Thank goodness everything went well.'

Frankie sipped the drink, appreciative of the cool breeze that drifted up from the ocean. 'Her daughter Rose lives with Eli, in my little flat on the Gold Coast. They're both doing well at uni and they're coming to visit just after Christmas. We're so excited to introduce them to Charlotte.'

'What about your other daughter?' Bert asked Simon. 'I haven't seen her since she left.'

Simon's eyebrows lifted high on his forehead. 'That's because she's never come back. I tried a lot over the years to get her to visit but her mother talks her out of it. She's grown up in Cairns and has been spoilt rotten. She rings me every so often when she has an argument with her mother. She's asked me for money a couple of times. I don't really know her anymore.' He looked across the water, pointing to a sailing boat that meandered across the bay. 'What can you do? I can't force her to visit.'

Bert followed his gaze. 'There might be a few of those boats heading this way. There's a bit of wild weather coming.'

'A cyclone?' Frankie asked.

'No, just some rain and wind. Surely, we'll have to get a cyclone soon though. We're well due one,' Bert said, offering Myrtle's glass to her, trying to get her to drink something.

Myrtle hadn't taken her eye off Charlotte and she pushed Bert's hand away. She looked confused as if she was trying to work out who the baby was.

'Myrtle was the best mother to our kids. They all think the world of her and visit regularly. We have five. Not a day goes past when one of them doesn't ring to talk to her or see how she is. She doesn't often talk back on the phone, but she likes to listen. Don't you, Myrtle?'

Myrtle nodded and then held out her hands towards Frankie.

Nobody spoke and Frankie hesitated for a moment. 'Would you like to hold Charlotte?' she asked.

Myrtle didn't respond but continued to hold her hands out.

Frankie stood up and came to stand beside the older lady. She looked at Simon, who nodded. Bending down she gently placed the sleeping Charlotte in Myrtle's arms.

Myrtle relaxed back in her chair and nestled the baby in next to her. She rocked her gently, back and forth, her eyes never leaving Charlotte's face. Simon resumed the conversation and the three of them sat talking, the sound of Myrtle singing to the baby, a soothing gentle sound.

They watched Myrtle as she sang. For a moment it seemed that her worries were gone, her forehead which was usually lined with creases, relaxed and her eyes no longer flitted back and forth as she tried to work out who was who or what was going on around her. Her shoulders sank back into the chair and she crossed her legs casually, a picture of elegance as if she'd done it all a hundred times before.

It was amazing how she could remember all the words for the nursery rhymes, and lyrics for songs that she rattled off one after the other. Tears filled her eyes and Frankie became emotional also, wondering what thoughts were going through the older lady's mind.

When Bert stood up, Myrtle seemed to know it was time to go. She stopped her singing and kissed Charlotte's forehead lightly. She looked up at Frankie. 'Put some baby oil on her scalp, it will get rid of the cradle cap and stop eating plums, you're giving her wind.'

With that, she stood up and passed Charlotte back to Frankie, a final stroke of the baby's face with her finger before she linked her arm through Bert's. Bert shook his head and closed his eyes. 'We are always amazed at how she can remember different things, yet not others.' Bert tested her. 'What's my name, Myrtle?'

She frowned, the creases in her forehead returning, her eyes wide as she stared hard.

She pulled a funny face. 'I don't know your name, but you're very handsome and one day I'm going to marry you and walk up the aisle.'

CHAPTER 7

As the heat of summer intensified, Frankie spent most of her time inside the house with Charlotte. Simon was around more than usual, working nearby. He'd been a solid help in the first few weeks. After all, he'd done it all before. The opening of the door when he came home from work was music to Frankie's ears and she'd pass the baby to him, telling him everything that had happened while he had been at work. Simon was also besotted by Charlotte and shared the load of the million and one things that needed doing. It was a luxury to have a break from feeding and nursing, a short time to have a shower and put clean clothes on, even ten minutes by herself.

There was no rush though and she loved every minute of the day. Charlotte was growing quickly and had started smiling as well as making those gorgeous baby noises that melted their hearts. They were both smitten, and she enjoyed being at home and looking after Charlotte. Who would ever have known that a tiny baby could bring so much contentment and happiness?

It wasn't long after the birth that Frankie made a decision. 'I just can't stand the thought of leaving her,' she told Simon. 'I know when I was pregnant I said I'd go straight back to work but you said I didn't need to and I'm loving being at home. Do you think we'd be okay without my income? I don't think I could hand her over to someone else to look after. She's growing too fast and neither of us should miss any of it.'

Simon was delighted with her decision and sighed with relief. 'I was never really happy about you returning to work. I support anything you want to do and I understood that your career is important but ...' He picked Charlotte up cuddling her close. 'Nothing is as important as this.'

Frankie glowed with love. Her life was complete. It had gone in an entirely different direction than what she had ever imagined. She didn't care that she still carried weight from being pregnant, that her eyebrows needed plucking or her hair needed a cut and colour. Inside the house, clean washing was piled high on the lounge chair, and another load that had been folded sat ready to be put away. Dishes were left in the sink and the floor needed sweeping. None of it mattered. She had Simon and Charlotte. There was nothing else she needed.

* * *

Christmas came and went. There had been plenty of summer rain and everything was green and lush. Simon's tanks overflowed and the garden took on a new lease of life. It was a shame that he hadn't heard from his daughter, Amelia. She could have at least rung or sent a card for Christmas. He brushed it off. It had always been the same since her mother had left him and taken their daughter with her. Fortunately, Eli had remained living with him after the separation, although it had broken his heart that Amelia not only didn't want anything to do with him but also didn't want contact with her brother.

They'd often discussed the situation and Frankie had encouraged Simon to write or ring his daughter. It was important that he have some sort of connection with her. 'She doesn't reply to anything and her mother certainly doesn't. She's wiped me from her life I'd say. Maybe when she's an adult she might see things a bit clearer. It's a shame for Eli also, they were close as little kids,' Simon said. 'His mother never bothered with him after a while. I think he calls her at Christmas and on her birthday.'

'That's so sad,' Frankie said. 'At least Eli is close to you.'

Eli and Rose visited for two weeks after Christmas. They'd both grown up so much over the last couple of years and were enjoying uni life and doing well in their courses. Rose had topped her academic year group and been offered further scholarships and opportunities.

Just like his dad, Eli was smitten with Charlotte. He nursed her any chance he could and Frankie was sure he made extra noise to wake her, just so he could rush in and be the first to pick her up when she woke.

Rose watched him, laughing as he poked his head from behind the lounge, playing hide and seek and making all sorts of ridiculous noises to gain the baby's attention. Charlotte rewarded him with huge smiles each time he popped out and surprised her. She had two dimples and blue eyes that were the same as Simon's and Eli's. There wasn't enough hair to brush, but the black hair she had been born with had turned blonde and there were even a few wispy ringlets forming at the back. Everyone commented how much she looked like her dad and brother.

'I don't think I got a look-in,' Frankie said to Rose. She's the image of Simon and Eli.

Rose lay on the lounge, her slender legs stretched out along the cushions. 'Thank goodness you got new air-con in here. I've become soft from living down south. Yes, she does look like both of them. You'll have to have another one maybe, except this time try and get to the hospital. Poor old Mum. You nearly gave her a heart attack.'

'You wouldn't have known it at the time. She was so calm.'

'She's birthed a lot of babies for the mob up north. If you wanted someone with you to help, she's the person. I think someone was watching out for you that day.'

'Do you think you'll want babies in the future? I mean not now but when you're older,' Frankie asked, amused by the look of horror on Rose's face.

'Not likely. Not for a long time anyway.' Rose laughed. 'Look at Eli's face, you've scared him with even the mention of it.' Rose threw a cushion at him as he crawled around the floor, making meowing noises to entertain Charlotte. 'I spent half my life looking after the younger ones in my family. I was changing nappies when I was seven; real ones made from cloth, with pins that drew blood when your finger got in the way.'

Eli came and sat on top of Rose's legs, tickling her as

she squirmed underneath him. 'Rose reckons she's not having kids and I'm for that. Mind you,' he rolled his eyes at Frankie, 'I remember someone else who thought like that and now look at you.'

* * *

The two weeks flew past and before she knew it, Rose and Eli were preparing to leave. Simon was taking them to the airport and she stood on the stairs waving to them as they drove off through the gate. She thought about the first time she had come through that gate, remembering her impression of the house and yards. It had been an extra surprise when Simon had led her through the house and out along the path that led down to the beach.

The ocean had sparkled that day and she had called it the jewel sea, mesmerised by the dancing diamonds on its surface, the silver tinnies that sped across it and sting-rays that skimmed through the waves. The area had rekindled her passion for protecting the environment and the job she had landed with the council, working with the turtle breeding program, had fallen into her lap at exactly the right time.

She thought about those early days as she walked around the back of the house, shaking her head at Barney, who stood like a statue under the shade of the fig tree. They stared at each other, neither moving for a moment. When the flies on his back became too much he flung his head around to chase them. As he turned back towards her, the saggy fold of his neck swayed back and forth, one front leg stomping to chase away more flies. The huge hump protruding on the top of his neck showed that he was a Brahmin, and Simon had told her that, that particular breed was well suited to the conditions of the area. The bull's legs seemed small in comparison to the rest of his bulky body, his rump and stomach so solid and large that she wondered how on earth they supported the massive weight of his body.

Maureen said that he wouldn't hurt a fly but she wasn't sure about that. She wasn't going to get close enough to test that theory.

Reaching into her pocket she pressed some buttons, waiting for the ringtone and smiling as someone picked up at the other end of the line. 'Artie,' she said, using her most stern voice.

'Frankie, love, is that you?'

'Yes.'

'Not that black bull again. Is he paying you a visit? I've fixed that fence. He shouldn't be out.'

She didn't respond.

'Okay, I'm on my way, love. Won't be long.'

She hoisted Charlotte up more comfortably on her hip and laughed as she put her phone away and walked back into the house. She was starting to feel like a local.

By February the days were sweltering, the build-up of clouds on the horizon an ominous warning that rain was on its way. Simon had driven the tractor to one of the fields and Charlotte was asleep in her cot. Frankie just needed a few moments to take the washing in from the line. She went out through the back door, looking around the yard. It was clear, not a horse or bull to be seen. Maybe this time Artie had fixed the fence properly.

She dawdled as she took the clothes in, folding them as she went. It was still hot even though it was late in the afternoon, but she didn't mind and she took her time, enjoying being outside. Some weeds had poked their head up in her garden and she bent down, adjusting her wide-brimmed hat to make sure her face was protected. Even a short while in the sun without a hat in North Queensland could result in sunburn and she was always careful, especially in the hottest times of the day. Summer was far different than what she knew down south. The humidity soared some days to around one hundred percent and every bug imaginable was either flying around looking for someone to sting, or landing on her veggie patch, munching at something she was trying to grow.

The air was still today, with no breeze, and dark clouds hung on the mountains to the east of the farm. It was like the weather was building up, each day hotter than the last and the promise of the rainy season not far away.

Ocean currents that travelled along the tropical coast swirled further out, the warm moist air above the surface drawn up, creating the fuel needed to form the spinning clouds that would eventually form a cyclone. The Whitsundays had a strong history of cyclones and the people and buildings were prepared for such events. The thought of being in one made Frankie nervous though, particularly now they had Charlotte. Hopefully she wouldn't have to experience one. There were plenty of years when they received the monsoonal rain without the destructive winds and rain. It would be good to keep an eye on the weather though. Everyone seemed to be talking about it.

Charlotte had only just gone to sleep so she had an hour or so before she woke up. She'd just take a peek at the ocean before she went back inside.

The water was an aqua colour today, the reflections of the puffy white clouds mirrored back across its surface. Two sailing boats glided across the horizon, their sails billowing out behind, catching the breeze as they raced towards the point at the far end of the bay. A movement in the water not too far out caught her eye.

There was something splashing out there, something different than the usual sting ray or school of bait fish. Standing on her tiptoes she jumped with excitement as a whale breached the water, its spout clearly visible from where she stood. Its body rose above the waves as it plied its way south, splashing down again before disappearing under the surface. Whale season had finished and she was surprised to see a whale this late in the year. Shielding her eyes against the sun, she peered out across the ocean, searching for its movements, rewarded by a few more distant splashes before it was no longer visible.

She watched for a bit longer before turning and heading back to the house. There was still some time spare before Charlotte woke up and she wanted to get dinner ready for Simon. Tonight she'd make his favourite–fish curry–and she wanted it ready so they could eat early. This time of the year was busy on the farm and he was usually tired when he came home from work. By the time he cleaned up, played with Charlotte and had dinner, he was often ready for bed, worn out from long hot days in the paddocks.

Life had changed in a way she never thought possible. Her main concern these days was the baby and then dinner. As she bounded up the stairs she was thankful that she felt fit and that her figure had finally found its way back to its prior form, her slim body fitting back into her favourite tiny denim shorts and singlet tops.

Simon had commented on her body yesterday when he pulled her in tight for a kiss. 'You don't even look like you're thirty, let alone thirty-seven,' he said before pressing his lips down on hers, his hands wrapping around her waist. She was still thinking about where that kiss had led when she entered the house through the back door.

Charlotte would still be asleep, but she'd just check on her. As she walked through the lounge she noticed the front door was open. Strange, she always kept it closed; the air conditioning was on and the place needed to be shut up to keep the cool air in. A prickling sensation crept over her skin and she shrieked as she looked towards the entrance of Charlotte's bedroom. A young girl stood in the doorway. She was about fifteen and leaned back on the door jam, her arms crossed, a scowl on her face. Frankie froze, her voice loud as angry words tumbled out. 'What the hell do you think you're doing?'

The girl twisted her mouth up, a smirk on her face. 'Mum said some chick had moved in with Dad. She said there was a baby.'

Frankie straightened up, her mind reeling as she grabbed the girl's arm and pulled her away from the baby's room. 'How dare you walk into this house. Get out!' She pushed her out into the lounge room and rushed back to the cot to check on Charlotte, who squirmed a little before repositioning herself and settling back to sleep.

The girl flopped onto the lounge, her feet placed up on the coffee table, her eyes roving around the room. 'You do know who I am, don't you?' she asked.

Frankie stood in front of her, using her feet to kick the girl's feet off the table. 'I have a fair idea. I've seen photos of you when you were smaller. You're Amelia. Simon's daughter.'

The girl sat up, glaring straight back at her. 'It's Amy. I'm not called, Amelia, anymore.'

'Well, Amelia, or Amy, or whatever your bloody name is. You can't just walk in here without asking. How dare you.'

'Why not? It's my house and that baby is in my room.'

They stared hard at each other. Frankie's breathing returned to normal as she tried to assess the situation. Simon hadn't heard from his daughter for ages and he certainly hadn't mentioned that she might call in. It was definitely her though. She recognised her from photos Simon had shown her. There was also a strong resemblance to Eli. Long blonde hair hung from beneath a black beanie, dark eye makeup and black fingernail polish all matched, along with the dark clothes and heavy boots that she wore. A silver stud in her nose matched the three or four in each ear and Frankie thought how hot she must be in those clothes. Beneath the clothing and make-up, there was a resemblance to Eli but it was amazing how different they were in personality. She'd only just met the girl but that much was obvious.

'How did you get here?'

'I caught a taxi.'

Frankie picked up some of the toys lying around, pretending to be busy and nonchalant about her arrival. 'Look Amelia... Amy. We may have got off to a bad start. I was shocked to find someone in the house.'

Anger was written on Amy's face. 'It's my house also, don't forget that.'

She ignored the remark. 'Come into the kitchen and I'll get you a cool drink. You must be hot in those clothes.'

Amy curled her lips up in a fake smile, that dropped away just as fast as it had arrived. 'I wear them in Cairns.' She stood up, crossing her arms sullenly. 'When will Dad be home?'

'He can't be too far away. He will be surprised to see you.' Boy, will he be surprised, Frankie thought.

Amy got up and strode into the kitchen. 'Will he?'

'What would you like to drink? Coffee or a cold drink?'

'A beer will do,' Amy replied as she flopped into one of the kitchen chairs, tapping her fingers on the timber table as she looked around the room. 'Have you got an ashtray I can use?'

'You're not smoking in here and you're not old enough to have a beer.' Frankie placed a can on the table. 'Have a coke,' she said as she poured a small glass for herself. Soft drink was not something she usually drank, but she needed something to hang onto. The shock of finding a stranger in the house was unsettling and now this teenager, who it was hard to believe was Eli's sister and Simon's daughter, was rattling her even more with her arrogant attitude and surly face. She had trouble written all over her and she wondered if Simon knew that his little girl, Amelia, had turned into a goth-looking, troublesome teenager called Amy, who smoked cigarettes and asked for a beer at ten o'clock in the morning.

The sound of the front door opening brought relief and Frankie stood up and walked toward the lounge room as Simon came towards her. 'Hope you've got the kettle on. I'm dying for a strong cup of tea.' He leaned down and kissed her, pulling her in close, one hand wrapping firmly around her backside.

He'd always loved it when she wore her denim shorts. It reminded him of when they'd first met and he'd often said he found it difficult to keep his hands away from her when she had them on. As he squeezed her bottom, pressing her into his body, she tried to warn him that they had a visitor. Simon however had only had eyes for her and her denim shorts, only looking up when she pulled away from him.

'We have a visitor,' she mumbled, inclining her head toward the kitchen, where Amy sat directly behind the doorway, carefully watching the interaction that had just taken place.

The young girl didn't move, the can of coke in her hand, a detached nonchalant look on her face.

Simon stared hard, his eyes wide as the realisation of who was sitting at his kitchen table hit him. 'Amelia?' his voice was like a squeak. 'Amelia? What are you doing here?'

As she stood up she tipped the contents of the can of coke down her throat. When she finished, she placed it back on the table and turned toward him.

Fingers decorated with black finger-nail polish fidgeted and she pulled her beanie down lower, tucking stray bits of hair under its edges. 'I came to see you. I caught the train down from Cairns and then a taxi here.'

Frankie watched with interest as Simon placed his hat on the table. She thought that they'd hug, that Amelia would at least give him a cuddle. But they didn't, instead they both just stared at one another, neither making a move towards the other.

'So, you've met Frankie?' Simon said.

'Yep, we've met.'

Frankie smiled. 'Amelia, or Amy as your daughter now likes to be called, was inside the house, actually in Charlotte's room when I came back in from outside. I thought she was an intruder. She's lucky I recognised her from your photos.'

Simon's eyes narrowed. 'You should have rung or at least let us know that you were coming.'

Amy pulled a packet of cigarettes out of her pocket. 'I'm going outside for a smoke. Your girlfriend told me I can't smoke inside.'

Simon stood looking at the door as it shut behind Amy. His mouth open and closed a few times but no words came out. Frankie busied herself making morning tea. Her head was whirling as Simon's words came at her, hard and fast.

'What the hell? Are you telling me that you came in and she was in the house? Let herself in and didn't even ask. I'm so sorry, that would have given you a fright.'

'It did. Luckily I recognised her, well I thought it was her. She told me this is her house and she could come in whenever she wanted. I dragged her away from the baby's room. I thought she was going to hurt Charlotte.'

Simon opened the kitchen window and peered across

the yard. Confusion was written all over his face and he lowered his voice. 'She's too young to smoke and what's with the way she's dressed.'

'I don't know. You tell me. Here, take the coffee and go out and talk to her. Charlotte will wake up soon, so I'll stay in here.'

'Are you sure you don't want to come and talk to her also?'

She laughed. 'You're on your own buddy. That's your teenage daughter, not mine. Good luck with that.'

* * *

Frankie could see and hear through the open window and she watched curiously as Simon sat down next to Amy. She must be melting in the long black trousers and shirt she wore, the knitted beanie an odd piece of headwear for summer in the tropics. Simon obviously hadn't brought up the topic of putting the cigarette out as Amy continued to puff away, her beanie pulled down low on her head, her shoulders slouched. Her only visible response was when the two dogs bounded out from the bushes. No doubt they'd been over next door. So much for relying on them for guard dogs. Mango season was in full swing and both of them liked to steal Artie's fruit from his tree. They'd find the ones that had fallen on the ground and holding them between their paws, pull the skin off with their teeth. The flesh was sweet and succulent, the tropical fruit, a cool treat on a hot summer's day.

Artie didn't care, the tree was laden. His dog Riley usually joined them. Sometimes Maureen took a photo and sent it to her with a funny comment to let her know where they were.

Amy patted them as they pushed their noses into her hands. She'd been four when her mother had taken her and left. The dogs would have been pups back then. It looked as if they remembered her though and after they jumped all over her they lay at her feet, every so often getting up and pestering her until she rewarded them with a pat.

The sound of the conversation taking place drifted up through the open window and Frankie listened hard, intrigued at what they were talking about.

'It's good to see you Amelia, but you shouldn't be smoking. What would your mother say?'

Amy flicked the butt onto the dirt, squashing it with her boot. 'She doesn't care what I do. The other thing is I haven't been called Amelia for years. My name's Amy.'

Simon took a long sip from his cup. 'Okay, I can live with that. Amy, it is. Now about the cigarettes. You can't smoke here and you shouldn't be smoking at all.'

'Why not?' She looked up at Simon and even from afar Frankie could see the stubborn look on her face, the glint in her eye.

'Because I said so. We haven't seen each other in a long while so I'm interested in why you've just suddenly turned up and how long you're staying. You said you caught the train here. You should have called before you came. Surely your mother could have contacted me. You both have the number.'

Amy's voice was loud and both the dogs sat up when she answered. 'She doesn't know I'm here or that I've decided to move back with you. My backpack is on the front verandah. It's got my clothes and books in it.'

Frankie slumped down into one of the kitchen chairs. Perhaps she'd just heard that wrong. Had that dark clothed, insolent teenager just said she was moving back here? With Simon? Surely she couldn't mean back here to this house. How the hell was that going to work?

CHAPTER 8

A week had passed since Amy had arrived and it had been seven days full of arguments, yelling, and tantrums. Frankie watched with interest as Simon tried to navigate the surly behaviour and demanding ways of his teenage daughter. There had been lengthy discussions on the phone with his ex-wife, Yvette, who admitted that over the last year she had lost control of Amy. Even though she'd only just turned fifteen, she was used to going out and doing what she wanted and had now obviously decided that she wanted to live with Simon. It would be good for her to reconnect with her father and brother. Yvette had another new partner and they planned to travel, so it was for the best for everyone that Amy moved back to Dingo Beach.

It was the school holidays so Simon had a small amount of time up his sleeve to have the conversation with Amy, that she *would* be returning to school. The local high school had everything she needed and he'd get her to the main road in the morning and pick her up in the afternoon. A bus went past and she could use that to go back and forth. He told her she wasn't allowed to live back with him unless she agreed to those arrangements. She had relented on that matter, but Frankie wasn't fooled and wondered how long she'd last, catching a bus each day and going to a school where she wouldn't know anyone.

They'd cleaned out the spare bedroom and bought new furniture and a black rug – Amy's choice. Simon was perplexed when another argument blew up about him painting the room that would now be her bedroom.

'I like it the way it is. The walls look dirty, grungy. Just leave it.'

Frankie could tell his patience after a week was wearing thin. She'd tried to keep out of the arguments and had been as pleasant as she could, focussing her energy on Charlotte, the meals, and the housework. Her peaceful lifestyle, however, was shattered and the fact that Amy wanted nothing to do with her new baby sister or Frankie, was really starting to rub on her nerves. She understood Simon's predicament. As Amy's father, she was his responsibility and at this stage going back to her mother wasn't an option. There was no other choice.

Day after day he tried to please his daughter and develop some sort of relationship. When he spoke to her he kept his voice level and unruffled, trying to get her to see his point of view or what was the right way to act or talk. Diplomatic, cajoling and positive, and always calm. Frankie knew though that the frustration was simmering underneath. 'I don't mind your suggestions, Amy, but try and use some manners,' he said for the hundredth time. 'A, please, would be nice.'

When Amy spoke to Frankie, the young girl was disrespectful and often swore. She was a bit more polite when Simon was around, but when he wasn't there, she was rude, surly, and mean. Frankie tried to stay out of her way and avoided being in the same room. But Amy was always in the kitchen, helping herself to whatever was in the fridge and leaving dirty dishes and leftover food everywhere.

To give herself some space, Frankie started to go for walks in the late afternoon. Charlotte was big enough now to sit propped up in the pram and if they followed the grassy tracks that Simon had mowed along the boundary fence, she could get a decent walk in. After a circuit of the paddocks, they'd make their way to the beach where she could sit in the sand with Charlotte on her lap and watch the birds in the trees or the dogs running around. If Simon came home early he joined them. At the moment it was the only time they had alone where they could discuss the situation in private.

He was at a loss how to improve his relationship with Amy and it hadn't escaped him that she was also rude to Frankie. 'I just feel like I have a lot to make up to her,' he said. 'She's missed out on all the years that Eli had here with me. It seems though that every time I talk to her I end up lecturing her, and then it ends in an argument. Surely if she starts to enjoy living here and settles in at school, she'll become a nicer person.' Frankie raised her eyebrows, unsure how long that was going to take and if it would ever happen at all.

She thought about their conversation and the pressure that Simon had on him as she manoeuvred the pram over the grassy path. This afternoon the sky was clear and two eagles circled directly above as she made her way to the boundary fence. Here it was peaceful, with no arguments. Before she had left for the walk she had knocked on Amy's bedroom door and let her know she was going outside. Just because the surly teenager had no manners didn't mean Frankie also had to be rude.

Amy had been stretched out on her bed when Frankie put her head in through her doorway. As usual, she had her earplugs in, listening to music, her eyes closed. She spent a lot of time in her room, which was a blessing. Her response to Frankie was a couple of blinks of her eyes, letting her know she had heard.

It was a relief to get out of the house and even though it was stinking hot, Charlotte was shaded in the pram and didn't seem to mind the heat. Frankie's legs were tanned from being outside and her wide-brimmed hat protected her face from the heat of the day. It amazed her how Simon worked all day in it, the humidity up to ninety percent, the air, still and heavy with the sultry summer weather.

Tall cane lined the first track she walked down, the tops of the thick stalks colourful with pink flowers that stood still, no breeze to move them. Dark mountains rose behind the fields and the rumble of a tractor sounded in the distance. On the sides of the mountain, thick vegetation covered the slopes, the tops covered in tall trees, the gullies filled with scrub and bushes that were often impenetrable. She'd walked up some of those hills with Simon before she was pregnant. Together they'd climbed the highest one, standing on the summit under the shade of the tallest pine trees she'd ever seen. They reminded her of the trees that grew on the slopes of Gloucester

Island, their trunks often bent in one direction from the wind that blew in from the ocean.

The area had everything. Mountains, rainforest, fertile plains filled with cane, lush grasslands and to top it off the sparkling ocean, white beaches and scattered islands. It was a paradise and although the summer heat was stifling, she couldn't imagine living anywhere else. She had become more and more attached to the Whitsundays and the people who lived in and around the small towns that dotted the coastline. She'd made friends in Dingo Beach and nearby morning teas and yoga classes at the small village of Hideaway Bay had added to her group of friends. They'd welcomed her with open arms and fussed over Charlotte, reminding her that whenever she needed help, they were there. Just a phone call away.

The track she walked over was bumpy and Charlotte had fallen asleep. Frankie lay the pram down, tucking the light cover around the baby's legs, keeping the insects from biting her soft skin. Long eyelashes spread out across Charlotte's chubby cheeks and curly blonde hair lay tousled underneath her. She put her thumb in her mouth, her perfect little lips moving and sucking as she slept. Frankie tucked her fat little foot in under the cover. She was perfect. The most beautiful cuddly baby she'd ever seen. The sound of a vehicle coming along the path distracted her and she stood up, shielding her eyes from the sun. An orange tractor chugged towards her, Artie waving at her from the driver's seat.

He pulled up next to her and turned the tractor off, before getting down to talk. As usual he wore his blue shorts and khaki work shirt, his feet bare, his head covered with his tattered hat.

'How ya going, love?' he asked, as always a wide smile on his face. 'How's that beautiful baby?'

Frankie gave him a hug, ignoring his retorts that he was dirty and smelly. She had become attached to Artie and Maureen, and when they got together for morning tea as they sometimes did, they'd often had a good laugh together at her annoyance towards their black bull and drifting smoke when she'd first moved to the farm.

Frankie smiled as Artie bent over to look closely at the sleeping baby. 'She's sleeping and we're just out for our walk. How are you and Maureen?'

'Can't complain,' he said as he straightened up, his hand rubbing his belly. 'Every day you wake up is a good day.'

She laughed. He always had a funny saying or story to tell. Sometimes Maureen had invited Simon and Frankie over for drinks and by the time the night was over and they'd returned home, Frankie's stomach was sore from laughing so much.

He leaned back on the tyre of the tractor, his arms crossed. 'I hear young Amelia has come back to live.'

'She certainly has. We've cleaned the spare room out for her. Simon is making her start school later this month. She didn't want to but he's said she has to go to school if she wants to live with us.'

Artie ran his hand through his hair, before putting his hat back on. 'What's she like?'

She sighed. How could she even begin to explain the situation?

'What you're not saying is telling me something,' Artie said. 'Simon told me the other day that she's a right pain in the arse!'

'He's allowed to say that. I'm not. It's not been easy. She's rude to me and doesn't even acknowledge Charlotte. Common everyday rules mean nothing to her and she thinks she should be allowed to do whatever she wants.'

'Not what you'd counted on, hey. Your farm is not the paradise it once was.'

'No, Artie. It's not what either of us had counted on. But there's not much we can do about it. She's Simon's daughter and she wants to live with us, well him anyway. I'm not sure she wants to live with me or Charlotte.'

Artie crossed his arms, glancing down at his silver watch. He chuckled, 'And you thought my bull was a problem. Surely a wisp of a girl is easier than Barney.'

'Don't forget she's a teenager and she's been allowed to do whatever she wants.'

Artie lifted his hat off his head and ran his fingers through the small amount of hair that he had. 'There's no excuse for bad manners. Can I give you a bit of advice? I've got five grown-up daughters of my own and a mob of grandkids. I love them all to death but I'll tell you something.' He rubbed his stomach and looked at his watch again. It was probably getting near to his beer time. His words were slow and he spoke quietly. There was no rush in North Queensland and certainly not when you were in the cane fields having a chat.

He stood up, his eyes narrowing as he looked at her. 'Don't put up with any shit from her. You're Simon's partner and you've got a baby to look after. Put that Amelia in her place. That's your house and Simon's, you two are the ones paying the bills and looking after everything. It's not hers at all. She's just a kid and it sounds like she needs to pull her socks up. Put her in her place.'

She shrugged. 'Easier said than done. She's got no respect for anyone, not even Simon.'

'Agh, he'll be too soft. He feels responsible for not seeing her all these years. He's probably trying to make up to her for missing so much time when she was growing up.'

She thought hard. Artie was right, she'd seen Simon give in to Amy, time and time again, coaxing her with words and pussyfooting around the real issues. Yesterday, after Amy's persistent wheedling, he'd given her some money. They'd gone into Airlie Beach together and Amy had walked around the streets, looking at the shops while he was at the machinery store.

Frankie wanted to say something to him, to tell him that Amy would probably buy cigarettes with the money he'd just given her or waste it on unhealthy food or drinks. But she'd kept her mouth shut, not wanting to rock the boat any further than what it was already wildly swinging.

Artie patted her on the shoulder. 'I'm right, aren't I? Simon's a big softie, mind you so am I. But I'm telling you, you put that young one in her place. Don't give her an inch. Sooner or later, she'll buckle. Remember you're the boss.'

'Thanks, Artie. I must admit I've been trying to keep the peace and I've kept my mouth shut. That's getting harder though and I feel like I'm going to explode. Maybe I'll give your idea a go. I would love to put her in her place and get her to contribute or join in with us as a family.'

'Give 'em an inch and they'll take a mile.' He grinned at her as he started up the tractor, his hands swinging the steering wheel around. 'Beer time with my Maureen,' he called out, a final wave as he headed home.

Frankie walked slowly along the track, enjoying the last of the afternoon. Artie was right. She was in charge of the household. It was time to make a stand.

CHAPTER 9

hen Frankie returned from her walk, Simon was in the backyard throwing the ball to the dogs. He smiled and kissed her, reaching down to pick Charlotte up. She had just woken up and rewarded him with a smile, her chubby arms reaching up to his face. He nuzzled into her hands, her squeals of delight a playful sound as he tossed her into the air, catching her and smothering her in kisses.

'She's growing so quickly.' He put his arm around Frankie's shoulders and squeezed her tight. 'You look beautiful this afternoon. I don't know how you walk in the heat though, even this humidity is getting to me.'

She kissed him back. 'I love my afternoon walk. It gets me out of the house. I ran into Artie down near the side fence. He said to say hello.'

Their conversation was broken by the sound of the back door banging loudly. Amy pounded down the stairs an angry look on her face. 'I can't find my phone charger. Where did you put it?' She looked straight at Frankie.

Frankie glared back at her and went to reply but then paused. She turned back to Simon. 'Only time I've ever seen her move quickly is when she thinks her phone is going to die.' Taking a deep breath she turned back to Simon and continued talking, ignoring the angry teenager who stood with her hands on her hips, her black beanie low across her forehead.

'Are you deaf? I said, where's my charger?' Amy's voice bellowed out across the backyard.

"That's it,' Simon said to Frankie, his voice low so that Amy couldn't hear. 'I've had enough of her. This ends now.'

Frankie held his hand. 'No, she's talking to me. Let me deal with this. You can respond when she speaks to you rudely.'

Turning around Frankie took a step towards the stairs. Her voice was loud. 'Are you speaking to me, lovey?' she asked.

Amy rolled her eyes and crossed her arms, her stance insolent and sullen. 'Well, who else would I be talking to.'

Frankie smiled sweetly at her. 'Well, I don't answer rude people. When you're ready to be polite I might respond, but until then, go back inside, try and find your manners and don't interrupt your father and me when we're talking.' With that, she turned back to Simon, linked her arm through his, and led him down towards the beach.

Neither looked back, but from the sound of the back door slamming they knew Amy had returned inside.

* * *

They sat together in the sand, Charlotte propped in between Simon's legs. The sun had dipped behind the western mountains and a slight sea breeze cooled the area. The water was like glass, and tiny fish leaping across the surface sent rings of ripples across the top. A pink haze filtered across the horizon, and dark blue started to fill the sky. The evening star appeared above them, and a crescent moon became visible above the palm trees.

'Our paradise is not what it was a couple of months ago.' Simon sighed as he watched Charlotte try and grab the sand. 'Who would ever think that a cute little baby could grow into a monster that swears, is rude and doesn't care about anything except herself.'

'She's out of control,' Frankie replied. 'I've had a talk to Artie this afternoon. He said you told him she was a pain in the arse.'

Simon laughed. 'I'd just had an argument with her when I talked to him the other day. I did say that. I just don't have the patience for it. Eli was never like this. I'll tell her that if she doesn't lift her game she'll have to go back to her mother.'

'She has no excuse for the way she is and you've been more than patient with her.' She gave him a firm look. 'I've had enough. There's a line and she's crossed it with me. I'm not putting up with any of her antics, so be prepared for some arguments because I'm not giving in to her anymore and...' she put her hand up to stop him talking, 'I don't want you talking to her about being polite or nice to me. Let me deal with it, otherwise I'll never have any authority over her.'

'I'm so sorry she speaks to you the way she does. I talked to her about it but she won't listen.' He wrapped his arm around Frankie's shoulders. 'I'll support you all the way. You've got your hands full with Charlotte and dealing with the household. I'm worried if I flare up with her that she'll take off, to who knows where. She won't go back to her mother. I can't kick her out either. She's my responsibility and I'm trying to be firm.'

Frankie stroked his arm. 'Eli will be here in April and maybe by then she will have settled in. Perhaps school will help.'

Simon sounded defeated. 'Let's hope so.'

* * *

Every day was a new battle. When Amy was rude, Frankie ignored her antics or lectured her on how she should behave. When she complained about her dinner, Frankie quickly got up from the table, grabbed her plate and tipped it straight into the bin.

'What did you do that for?' Amy said. 'I hadn't finished my chips.'

'Oh, my goodness. I'm so sorry, I thought you said the salad tasted like shit.'

'I did, but the rest was okay. Now I've got nothing to eat.'

The arguments went on and on, and the only saving grace was that school had started. Simon had also become firmer with Amy and the house seemed to be in constant battle mode. Charlotte was starting to roll all over the floor, sleep less, and demand more feeds. It was tiring and the arguments were endless, but Frankie wasn't giving in. Amy was horrible and made it clear she didn't want anything to do with Charlotte. Frankie didn't trust her anyway. Amy's phone and music were a constant distraction so she wouldn't be any help even if she was in a good mood. As long as she stayed out of the way and kept her mouth closed, Frankie could get through the day.

Frankie had left it up to Simon to work out the school uniforms, books and resources. It had been a big enough battle to get Amy to agree to go to school, never mind to conform to a skirt and blouse, black shoes and no beanie. He'd finally sorted it all out after numerous trips into town with Amy in tow. 'At least she was polite to the uniform shop lady. I think she was happy that the skirt wasn't long like at her old school and they can wear black socks as well as white. She loves the colour black.'

'I'd love to throw that beanie out. She hand washes it herself and makes sure to bring it in from the line. Black. Who wears a black beanie in the middle of summer up here.'

'She'd be lost without it,' Simon said. 'Although the lady in the school office asked her to take it off when we went in for her interview. I'm not sure she'll be allowed to wear it at school. I just wish she would calm down and start being a decent person. You know, sometimes I get a tiny glimmer of her nice side.'

'Really. I've yet to see it.'

'When we drove home after getting her uniforms the other day she actually talked to me about my old records that she'd found in the cupboard. We discussed bands from years ago and she listened when I spoke about the music that I'd liked as a teenager. She even asked a couple of questions.'

'Wow, that's saying something. I never get anything from her except grunts.'

'Last week when she came with me on the tractor, she opened up a bit too. She told me she could remember sitting on my lap when she was little and driving through the cane on the tractor. We ran over a huge black snake and she has a clear memory of that. We talked about things that happened when she was little and I told her some stories about funny things Eli and her used to do. We also discussed the books she's been reading.'

'I noticed she takes books out of your bookcase. All those old Wilbur Smith and Bryce Courtenay ones. I wouldn't think they would be her taste, but I see them open on the lounge sometimes.' Frankie finished feeding Charlotte and passed her to Simon. 'I've tried to talk to her, to form some sort of relationship, but I'm not getting anywhere. She doesn't want anything to do with me.'

'She said she's made friends at school. Some of them are from Dingo Beach so at least they're local kids,' Simon said.

'I wonder who they are. You generally know everyone around the district. I hope they're nice.'

It wasn't long after that conversation that Frankie was introduced to Amy's 'friends'. She'd just put Charlotte to sleep one day when her phone rang. It was the principal, Mr Mackle-Penny, and he needed her to come and pick Amy up from school. Along with some other students she had been caught with marijuana behind the sports shed. The consequence was a suspension. She needed to be picked up immediately. Yes, they understood that Frankie had a baby and that it took an hour to drive in, but they couldn't have Amy there for the rest of the day. Rules were rules.

'Shit,' Frankie said out loud after she hung up. Amy

had only been at the school for a few weeks. What sort of friends had she made and where had the dope come from? It was bad enough that she smoked cigarettes and that she was possibly responsible for some of the wine that had gone missing from Simon's bottle rack.

Rose's mother, Cecily, had rung straight after the principal. She asked if Frankie could bring her youngest son, Jeremy, home too. He had been caught with Amy and the others. Cecily was without a car as it was getting fixed. She sounded furious. 'I'm going to throttle that boy. He's supposed to start this year off on a better foot than the last one. I'm at my wit's end regarding what to do with him and it's another month until his father is back from the mines. I've given the school permission to let him come home with you.'

Frankie sympathised with Cecily's angst, feeling her own anger building as she collected up what she needed and made her way to the car.

Trying to put Charlotte in her car seat without waking her up wasn't an easy task. She'd wriggled and opened her eyes the minute the straps clicked into place. That morning she'd been a bit cranky anyway and she'd only got her down for her morning sleep just before the phone call. The baby's room was air-conditioned and Charlotte had been in a heavy sleep, the room lovely and cool. Now she had to sit in a hot car seat and be placated with a bottle that would hopefully keep her happy for the drive into town. Singing along to music on the radio, Frankie tried to block out Charlotte's crying as she swung the car onto the highway and drove towards Proserpine. She was too young to be trying to bring up a teenager, she was only just working out what to do with a baby. There wasn't even any use ringing Simon about the incident. The sun hadn't even been up when he left this morning. He'd gone with some of the nearby farmers to the sale yards and wouldn't be back until late. This time she would have to deal with the problem herself.

* * *

Frankie paced up and down in the school foyer, juggling a tired and cranky Charlotte on her hip. A middle-aged office woman peered over the top of her glasses at her from behind the counter. 'You're, Frankie, are you? Here to collect Amy and Jeremy?'

'Yes, that's right.'

'Just a moment, please. I'll bring them out.' She handed over some paperwork, the bored look on her face letting Frankie know that she'd seen it all before. 'Suspension papers,' she said. 'Make sure you sign them, here, here, and here. They must be returned before Amy comes back. You'll also need to book a session with the guidance officer.' She peered over her glasses again. 'That would be for Amy and whoever is her guardian, or parent.'

Frankie smiled as if she wasn't worried about any of these matters. 'That will be her father, Simon, not me. I'll make sure I pass all the information on to him. He's at the saleyards …' Her last words were lost on the office lady who had turned and was already answering a phone. Just another day at the office, Frankie thought. Nothing special, just a bit of marijuana and a couple of suspensions. Simon was not going to be happy about this.

* * *

The principal escorted Amy and Jeremy out of his office. He shook Frankie's hand and introduced himself. His voice was deep, his face stern. 'G'day. I'm Mr Mackle-Penny. I spoke to you on the phone. You're listed as a carer and Amy said to ring you rather than her father as he was out of town.'

'Yes, that's right.'

Mr Mackle-Penny turned his gaze to Jeremy and Amy who both stood quietly, Jeremy looking at his feet and Amy peering out the window as if she didn't care less. 'Amy said you'd come and get her,' he said.

Frankie changed Charlotte's position to her other hip, trying to juggle the paperwork, a bottle, and the baby as she listened. 'As Amy is new to the school and this is her first infringement, we'll keep the suspension to three days. These two say they weren't actually smoking the marijuana but just happened to be with the others who were.' He held his hand up to silence Amy who had started to butt in. His voice was deep and stern, making even Frankie pull her shoulders up straight and listen. He frowned at Amy. 'Silence, young lady. You're in enough trouble as it is. Now as I was saying. The others were smoking it, but they've all agreed that these two were smoking cigarettes, not the dope and after conversations with them I'm going to take their word on it this time. Next time they get caught though it will be a much longer suspension and if the behaviour continues,' he coughed and adjusted his glasses, 'they will be expelled. We have very strict policies on drugs and a second infringement will not be tolerated.'

Jeremy hung his head, his eyes downcast. He was the same age as Amy, his black hair falling over his face, dark brown eyes finally looking up at Frankie, who gritted her teeth and glared at both of them. Charlotte started to cry as the principal continued his lecture, reminding them of the rules and consequences and also the damage they were doing to their education and future job prospects. He focussed on Jeremy. 'You have a great future with your dancing, Jeremy. Same as your brothers before you had with their sport. Look at what your sister Rosie has achieved. You can do the same. Don't mess it up. You're due to represent the school next month in the state creative awards, so I want you back here, backside on seat and focussed after this suspension is done. Do I make myself clear, young man?'

Jeremy looked up at the principal, his face stony as he pulled himself up straight. 'Yes, Sir. I didn't even have a smoke. I told you that. I keep fit so I can dance. I was just down there because Amy's new. I don't smoke cigarettes or dope.'

'Well, son, I've told you time and time again. If you lie down with dogs, you'll get up with their fleas.'

Amy pulled a face and scowled directly at the principal, who raised his eyebrows and glared back at her. 'You have a lot to learn Miss White. You might have got away with this at your last school, but we run a tight ship here and don't put up with any rubbish. I'd be careful if I was you. There aren't too many options around here. We're the only high school for a hundred kilometres so if you don't fit in here there aren't any options close by. You'll be spending every day at home.'

By now Charlotte was really starting to wind up, Mr Mackle-Penny's deep voice had frightened her and her crying became louder as she squirmed in Frankie's arms.

88

Bouncing her up and down she tried to placate her so that she could hear what was being said. Perhaps Charlotte also sensed the tenseness in Frankie's body as she listened to the principal's words, particularly the 'every day at home' part. That was enough to make anyone cry. Mr Mackle-Penny appeared oblivious to the fact that Charlotte was making so much noise and much to Frankie's dismay he continued talking, ignoring the racket that now filled the office.

'If you could make a meeting, Mrs White, for when Amy returns. I'd like to discuss some other options for her. The music teacher tells me she's a talented musician and singer. She's only been in the class for a couple of weeks but already she's standing out as someone with lots of talent. Miss Bryce said she's hoping that you try out for the school musical, Amy.'

Frankie was shocked. She hadn't heard Amy sing or play an instrument. She hadn't brought any with her. She turned to Amy, raising her voice to be heard over Charlotte's noise. 'Mr Mackle-Penny is talking to you. It's polite to reply.' She glared as hard as she could, feeling a slight sense of success when Amy managed to answer with a short comment.

Frankie shook hands with the principal and followed Amy and Jeremy out the door. The office lady watched them go no doubt thankful that they had, along with the screaming baby, left the building.

Tension hung in the air as they walked to the car and Frankie tried to juggle her bag, paperwork and Charlotte as she fumbled in her pockets for the car keys. 'Here let me take her,' Jeremy said, holding his arms out to take Charlotte. Frankie hesitated and narrowed her eyes at him as he spoke again. 'I'm good with babies. I've looked after heaps. I won't drop her.'

She passed him Charlotte who stopped crying immediately, her chubby hands clinging onto Jeremy's arm as he bounced her up and down. Charlotte looked up at the birds that he pointed to and smiled when he pulled funny faces at her. He laughed as she reached up and touched his face. 'What's her name?' he asked. 'She's so cute. You never told me you had a sister, Amy.'

A super scowl was fixed on Amy's face. 'She's not my sister.'

'Really.' Jeremy laughed, 'you're kidding aren't you? She's the spitting image of you. Look at her, the only difference is that she smiles.'

'She's Amy's half-sister and her name's Charlotte.' Frankie watched as Jeremy gently placed Charlotte in the car seat, buckling her in and hopping in beside her, making sure she was occupied the whole time and not crying. 'We always have babies at home. Mum looks after them for all the cousins. You're lucky, Amy, to have her to play with. I play with my cousins' kids for hours. They're heaps of fun.' He tickled Charlotte's feet, counting her toes with his fingers and talking to her as they drove back towards Dingo Beach.

Amy sat in the front seat, turning around every so often to look at Jeremy. Frankie kept an eye on him in the rear-vision mirror. He seemed to be pleasant enough and twice she saw him wink at Amy from the back seat. Clearly, the two of them had become friends in the short amount of time they'd been at school and if she wasn't mistaken Amy smiled back at him a few times and even laughed when he made Charlotte giggle.

'That's interesting that you talk about your mum and babies,' Frankie said.

'Why's that?' Jeremy asked.

She cleared her throat. 'Your mum delivered Charlotte for me, right in the middle of the cane fields and right about where you're actually sitting on the back seat right now. Whoever thought five months ago that I'd be driving her son and Simon's daughter home from school after they'd been suspended for drugs!' She smiled at Amy and shook her head. 'The world works in mysterious ways.'

Jeremy leaned forward between the two front seats. 'Oh my God. I remember Mum coming home and telling us all about that. She needed to have a strong cup of tea that afternoon. I hadn't made the connection. Don't you think that's incredible, Amy, my Mum brought your sister into the world. Bloody amazing.'

Amy giggled. 'It's a bit gross really. Having a baby in the back seat of a car. Where was Dad?'

'He was there, helping me through it. It was a nightmare. We were on our way to the hospital, but Charlotte just started coming, in the middle of nowhere. Your dad's phone had no reception and we'd stopped because once that baby starts wanting to get out it's not like you can tell it to wait. Thank goodness, Jeremy's mum was driving out to bring me eggs and honey. It was fate, a present from above. I'm not sure what would have happened if she hadn't come along because Charlotte's cord was around her neck and your mum helped me do the right thing to deliver her safely, right here in this car.'

'Mum has helped lots of babies come into the world. You'd die laughing if you could hear some of the stories I've heard about women when they're in labour. Our mob don't always like the men being there and mum has some funny stories about things they say when they're in a lot of pain.'

Frankie laughed. 'I can relate to that. It's sort of like something overcomes you and you turn into a different person.'

'How painful is it?' Amy asked, her face screwed up as she looked at Frankie.

Frankie shuddered. 'Really painful. Like you want to die.'

Amy winced and turned to look back at Charlotte. 'I'm never having kids. It sounds revolting and I hate pain.'

Frankie turned her eyes back to the road. 'Wasn't my plan either. I was happy being child-free. I was going to get a pup. No kids for me. Not in my plans.'

Jeremy added in. 'Look at her now. She's the most gorgeous baby I've ever seen. I'd sit and play with her all day. I bet you think differently now than when you thought you were never going to have kids?'

'That's wise of you to work that out, Jeremy. You're right. As soon as she was born, my whole world changed. That's why I've stayed at home with her instead of going back to work. I love being a mum, and your dad, Amy, is a good dad. He would have been the same with you and Eli.'

'I wish I could remember more. I was so little when we left.' Amy turned and looked out the window, her face downcast, her beanie pulled lower on her face.

'My mum's usually the mum and dad all in one,' Jeremy said. 'Dad's always worked away so much that she's had to do more than most mothers. Now we're all older we help her so it's got a bit easier for her. Dad's good when's he here and sometimes she goes away for a few days by herself to clear her head when he comes back. She says it does him good to be with us just by himself.'

'Do your mum and dad fight when he's home? My mum and her boyfriend are always arguing. I can't stand it. That's why I left,' Amy said.

Frankie listened intently. That was the first she'd heard of that.

'Nah, they still love each other. My dad calls her his little angel. It's embarrassing. They still hold hands when they walk along the beach. Sometimes I think my mum *is* an angel. She would do anything for us kids.'

'Well, she didn't sound too happy when she rang me,' Frankie said, watching Jeremy's face fall.

'You probably don't believe me because you don't know me, but I don't smoke or drink. I've seen what it does to people and I like being fit and healthy. Mum will listen to me though. If I've done something wrong I'd own up to it. I don't lie.'

They were nearly back to Dingo Beach when Amy spoke again. Charlotte had fallen asleep and Jeremy also had his eyes closed. 'Aren't you going to lecture me about what just happened at school? Ask me if I smoked dope or not?' Amy said.

Frankie smiled sweetly at her. 'That's not my job. That will be up to your father.'

Frankie advised Amy that it would be best if they didn't tell Simon what had happened until the following morning. He wouldn't be home until late at night and they'd all be asleep by then, so it was better to wait until the morning. 'He'll be tired and just want to go to bed when he gets home. It can wait until the morning, at least then he'll be thinking clearly.'

Amy's attitude had returned to its usual mopey demeanour, and she made some sort of noise, like a grunt, in response, before disappearing into her bedroom.

* * *

Breakfast was well underway when Simon joined Frankie and Charlotte at the kitchen table. He gave them a kiss each before taking the cup of tea that Frankie passed him. 'It was a big day yesterday so it's good to have a bit of a sleep-in this morning. Where's the grumpy one?' he asked. 'She'll miss the bus if she doesn't get out here soon.'

Frankie stood up and went to Amy's door, knocking loudly. 'Time to get up. Amy. Get out here now, you need to talk to your father.'

'What does she need to ask me now?' Simon's brow furrowed, his shoulders sagging in anticipation of whatever request was about to come.

Frankie sat down beside him. 'She got into trouble at school yesterday. Her and Cecily's son, Jeremy. They were with some others who were smoking dope. Apparently they weren't, Amy was smoking cigarettes and Jeremy was just with them. Anyway, they've suspended both of them for three days. I had to go and pick her up. We didn't bother you because we knew you were too far away. It was quicker for me to go and get her. I'll let her tell you the rest when she gets out here.'

'Jees, it's just one thing after the other with her.'

'Yes I had a lovely conversation with Mr Mackle-Penny. A lecture really and a very serious warning that if it happens again she'll be expelled. Do you know what that means, Simon? She would be stuck at home here with me. I'm not sure I could cope with that.'

'What did you say to her? Have you talked about it with her?'

'No, I've said not much at all. Actually, I steered away from asking her what happened or telling her what I think. That's your job.' Frankie got up and knocked on the door again. 'Get out of bed, Amy. Now!'

The door finally opened, and Amy dragged herself over to the table. Her eyes were dark, her hair messy and her clothes hung loosely around her slim body.

Simon sat back in his chair and folded his arms. 'I believe you've got something to tell me.'

Amy mumbled, her face grumpy, her eyes downcast. 'She's already told you anyway. So, you know.'

Simon's voice was deep and loud. 'She, is Frankie, and if you're rude one more time in this house or anywhere else, I'm going to pick up that phone and get your mother to come and pick you up. I've had enough of your disrespect, now sit up, get your hair back from your face and tell me what's going on.'

'Nothing.'

'Don't tell me that it's nothing.' He reached over and took her phone, her hand hovering over it, as usual. 'I'm hanging onto this until you start to behave like a normal person.' He held it up in the air when she tried to take it away from him. He shouted, making Frankie jump and Charlotte start crying. 'Sit down and stop with your disgusting attitude. This is it, Amy. There's a line and you've crossed it. Sit down and shut up.'

You could have cut the air with a knife and Frankie picked Charlotte up and bounced her on her lap. She could have left the room and left Simon to finish the argument, but she wasn't going to miss this showdown for the world.

'You can't take my phone from me.'

'Oh, yes I can, and I just did. It's my money that's paying for the calls and you're only fifteen and I'm your father and you'll bloody well do what you're told.'

A sullen silence ensued. Charlotte had smiled at all of them, and Frankie tried to keep a straight face as Charlotte reached out and tried to touch Amy who was sitting next to her.

'Now, I'm asking you to tell me what happened and

what you're going to do about it. I hope that you have the guts to tell me the truth.'

Amy sat up straight, her eyes blazing. 'Okay, so I got caught with the others. I wasn't smoking pot though, just cigarettes. You can ask Jeremy, he wasn't either. He doesn't even smoke cigarettes. I know you won't believe me, but it's the truth. If I'd been smoking pot, which is no big deal anyway, I would just say so.'

Simon looked at Frankie. 'I know you don't want to be involved in this but what do you think? You picked them up and talked to the principal. Are they telling the truth?'

Frankie took her time to answer, sipping her tea slowly and wiping some food from Charlotte's face before replying, as if she had all the time in the world. 'It seems they are telling the truth. The others all said the same and Amy told me she wasn't. Jeremy was very clear that he wasn't and that he wouldn't bother lying. I'm inclined to believe them.'

'See,' Amy said, sitting up even straighter, obviously pleased to think Frankie was on her side.

'Well, if Frankie believes you and I'd like to think you're telling the truth, we'll leave it at that. We do have to talk about the consequences though. The fact was you're not allowed to smoke at school so you've broken the rules anyway. It also sounds like you've got in with a bad crowd right from the start. I'll need to think about what to do with you over the next few days. There's no way you're just going to stay here and enjoy the solitude of your bedroom and music.'

Frankie passed Charlotte to Simon, busying herself collecting the dishes and making another cup of tea. 'Perhaps Amy and Jeremy could work on the farm for the next few days. That would give them both something to do, plus it would help you out.' It would also give me some peace and quiet here, she thought to herself.

Amy looked shocked, no doubt she had expected a lecture about keeping away from Jeremy, or instructions about doing schoolwork for the next few days.

Simon thought for a while. 'I could do with some help this week. What's this Jeremy like though, he sounds like a heap of trouble?'

Amy interjected and there was a slight sign of enthusiasm in her voice. 'He's really nice and he does the right thing. He doesn't usually hang around those kids we were with, it's just I wanted to have a smoke and he came down with us. He'd work hard and I could help too. If I work for you, can I have my phone back?'

Simon took his time, sipping his cup of tea and bouncing Charlotte on his lap. 'Of course, you can.' Amy smiled broadly, her face falling however as Simon continued. 'Absolutely. After the three days that is.'

CHAPTER 11

*C*ecily arrived with Jeremy early the next morning. Frankie hugged her warmly, ushering her into the house. 'Would you like a cup of tea, Cecily? Simon's just getting ready, he'll be out here soon.'

'That'd be great, love. Make it strong and three sugars,' Cecily said as she sat down at the kitchen table. She held her arms out to nurse Charlotte, the little girl rewarding her with a smile. 'She's grown so much,' Cecily held her in the air. 'What a beautiful baby.'

Jeremy pulled a chair out and sat down next to his mother. 'She's so cute and looks a lot like Amy.' He tickled Charlotte's feet as Cecily passed her over and placed her on his lap. 'You can nurse her while I have my cuppa.'

Frankie placed some cups on the table, talking to Cecily as she put the milk and sugar down in front of her. 'Simon will keep Jeremy and Amy busy for the next three days. He's not happy about Amy getting into trouble when she's just started at the school.'

Cecily's eyebrows raised high. 'He's not the only one

who isn't happy.' She glared at Jeremy. 'That school's looked after all my kids. The other boys excelled at footy and athletics. Jeremy has a natural talent for dance. He's hoping to get into the Bangarra Dance Group one day. Those teachers work hard to teach him and they reckon he's got a good chance. Mind you,' she scowled at him, 'he'll stuff up everything if he gets into trouble. Wait until Rosie hears about it, she'll be on that phone and giving it to him.'

Jeremy shook his head. 'I told you Mum, I wasn't smoking. I don't touch anything like that.' He sat up straight, a cheeky grin on his face. 'My body's a temple. Look at these muscles. I look after myself.'

'Full of himself, he is. You needs a good clip over the ears, boy. You watch yourself this week. I'll be checking if you've been doing what you're told. Don't think I've just forgotten about this. Poor Frankie having to pick you both up.'

Jeremy smiled back at his mother. 'Love ya, Mum.' He bounced Charlotte, turning her around to see Simon who had just walked into the kitchen.

Simon's voice was loud and cheery as he touched Cecily on her shoulder. 'Good morning. You're both here bright and early.'

Jeremy stood up and put his hand out in greeting, Charlotte positioned comfortably on his hip. 'Good morning, Simon. I'm Jeremy.'

Simon reached out and shook his hand as he took Charlotte from him. 'Pleased to meet you. It's good to finally meet one of Amy's friends. Talking about Amy, where is she?'

Frankie poured tea into the cups, peering down the

hallway to see if Amy was making her way out to them. 'I told her to be ready by six,' Simon said. 'Looks like I'll have to get her moving.' He stood up and walked towards her room.

Cecily relaxed back in her chair. 'How's it all been going? Wouldn't be all smooth sailing having a teenager back living with you. I suppose an extra set of hands would be a help with the baby though, if nothing else.'

Frankie lowered her voice. 'Not really. Amy doesn't have anything to do with Charlotte.' She smiled sweetly at Cecily. 'It's been interesting to say the least. Yesterday was really the icing on the cake for me.'

Simon reappeared, a disgruntled Amy not far behind him. As usual she wore dark jeans and a black t-shirt, her black beanie pulled down over her hair. Her face lit up when she saw Jeremy, and Frankie nearly spilled her tea as Amy greeted him with a smile and a chirpy good morning.

Cecily slapped her knee and laughed out loud. She made no secret of looking Amy up and down, her final look focussed on her beanie. Cecily's voice was loud and cheery as she greeted her. 'You must be Amy.'

'Yep.' Amy replied, leaning over to help herself to the toast that Frankie had just placed on the table.'

'That's the strangest work get-up I've seen in a while,' Cecily said, a few chuckles coming out in between her words. 'You'll swelter out there today, honey. It's going to get up to forty degrees.'

Amy glowered back at her, chewing slowly on her toast before answering. 'I don't have anything else to wear.'

Cecily folded her arms, looking straight at her. 'My

girls have extra clothes at home. I'll bring you some tomorrow.'

'Don't need any clothes, thanks. These are fine.'

Simon glared at her. 'Watch your manners, Amy. If this keeps up you won't be getting your phone back for a while. Consider another day added on for being rude to Cecily.'

She scowled back at him. 'That's my property. You can't keep it.'

Simon passed Charlotte back to Jeremy. 'Watch me. Just watch me. Now hurry up and finish. I've got plenty for you both to do.'

Frankie watched the interactions with interest, grateful that the conversation had turned from the usual daily arguments with Amy to discussing how Rose and Eli were going at university. Rose had phoned Frankie last night, appreciative that they had agreed to let Jeremy work on the farm for a few days. He was a good kid, she said, just easily led and like most kids that age, up for a bit of fun that often led to trouble. He was a talented dancer though and the family hoped that he'd be able to follow his passion and continue dancing once he left school. It was unfortunate that he and Amy had got caught up in the incident at school, but Rose hoped that it was a one-off. 'Don't worry, I'll be on the phone with him tonight. I'll let him know what I think about mixing with the wrong crowd,' Rose said.

Jeremy looked very much like his sister. He had dark skin and huge brown eyes, surrounded by long lashes. He was fit looking, as he'd announced earlier, and Frankie wondered if Amy had a crush on him. She definitely smiled more when he was around and had shown a nicer side of her personality in the car yesterday when he was there. Now she talked to him again, no snarling, no nastiness, and even laughing when he held Charlotte up in the air and recited a nursery rhyme. Hmmm, perhaps there was more to this friendship than Frankie had thought. Simon was in for an interesting three days and it made for some quiet time for her and Charlotte. She'd have the house to herself and no sulky teenagers to argue with.

* * *

Simon agreed that the first day had indeed been interesting. Amy had nearly passed out from heat exhaustion and spent most of the time under a tree at the side of the paddock trying to cool down. She'd been unimpressed when she had to walk through mud to move irrigation equipment and swore loudly when she'd fallen over and landed in cow manure. Jeremy on the other hand had been a great help. He could drive a tractor, untangle fencing wire and didn't need to be asked to do things. He knew how to move cattle and pre-empted what needed to be done. He seemed to be a step ahead all the time and worked hard all day. Best of all he kept the mood light and cheery, livening up Amy and keeping her going all day without too much sulking or complaining.

At lunchtime he'd entertained them with stories about his large family. It was obvious that his dad, who worked in the mines, was away a lot, and the child-rearing had been left to Cecily. 'You wouldn't want to talk back to my mum how you talked to Frankie this morning,' he told Amy. 'You'd get a mouthful, maybe a clip across the ear and for sure you wouldn't speak like that again.'

Simon watched the communication between the two teenagers. Amy appeared to listen to Jeremy without rolling her eyes or replying with sarcastic remarks. When they started to talk about music and bands they wanted to see, Jeremy had plied Simon with questions about the music he'd grown up with. Before long the three of them were chatting about different musicians and songs they loved. Amy relaxed and showed the pleasant side of her personality. She'd even rolled her jeans up at one stage, tossing her boots off and wriggling her toes in the dirt. Simon noted that she hadn't even taken out her cigarettes which she'd put in her backpack before they left the house.

He relaxed a little, enjoying the conversation and wishing that his daughter could be more like this when she was at home. Especially when she was around Frankie. A wave of guilt passed over him. He'd hardly been able to give Frankie any attention with everything else going on. Considering the unplanned pregnancy and frightening delivery, she'd come into her own in her new role as a mum, far better than both had ever imagined. Now she also had to contend with a teenager whose main aim seemed to be making her life as difficult as possible.

He needed to take her out, wine and dine her, and bring some romance back into their lives. Perhaps Cecily would come and babysit. She was always looking for ways to make extra money and he could pay her well and maybe she'd come for the weekend. He could take Frankie away for a night. Give her a break from Charlotte and more importantly, Amy.

CHAPTER 12

The three days passed without too much drama. The complaints from Amy had dwindled and then stopped and eventually she even become useful. Whatever she was usually grumpy about was forgotten and it was two days now since the black beanie had been seen. The heat had forced her to be practical and she'd also worn some of the clothes Cecily had dropped off for her. She looked like a completely different girl.

Her old self re-surfaced, however, when she resumed school and Jeremy was no longer by her side. Had it all been a show for him, perhaps she had a split personality, Frankie thought. Clothes once again covered her bedroom floor, her dishes with hard food on them littered the table and when Frankie tried to get her to clean up her mess she had yelled back at her. Simon had come home to his daughter arguing, shouting, and slamming her bedroom door so hard that the house shook. Thank good-ness Cecily had agreed to come the following weekend and look after Charlotte. Frankie needed a break.

* * *

It was a strange feeling to wave goodbye to Charlotte. Frankie had no qualms about leaving her in the care of Cecily who reassured Frankie that she wouldn't let her out of her sight. 'I've looked after plenty of babies in my day. You go and have some time to yourself and with Simon. God knows, you need it after putting up with that Amy. She won't want to give me any lip over the weekend.'

'Thanks so much Cecily. We do need some time by ourselves. I feel like we've hardly talked the last few months.'

'Your Simon is a good man. Go and enjoy yourself.'

'Hopefully Charlotte is good for you. I've expressed plenty of milk and it's ready for you in the bottles. Just ring if you need.'

'She'll be fine. Plus, you're only around the corner. Don't worry, I'll contact you if there are any problems, but there won't be.'

Simon had booked one of the cabins at the nearby Eco Resort at Cape Gloucester. The cabin was on the beach and Frankie was looking forward to eating at the restaurant and swimming in their pool. It was early March and the days and nights were sweltering. Heavy clouds hung low on the horizon and the forecasters were predicting cyclones for the weeks ahead. She had never experienced a cyclone and the stories the locals told her made her apprehensive about being in one. They assured her that the houses were built to endure the strong winds and Simon had done extra work on theirs to ensure it would withstand anything. Apparently, you couldn't lay claim to being a north Queenslander unless you'd been through a major cyclone.

Simon placed his hand on her leg as he drove out through the gate. 'Just you and me.'

'I know. It's exciting.' She grasped his hand, squeezing it as he gave her a cheeky grin. 'We haven't been away since before Charlotte was born.'

Simon looked back to the road in front. 'I've missed having you to myself.' He sighed. 'It will be good to get away from Amy for a while. You've been amazing, Frankie. Putting up with her rot.'

'I don't put up with it, really. That's why there are so many arguments. I won't back down. Hopefully one day she'll come good.'

'I occasionally get glimpses of a nice person underneath all the anger and rudeness. But it's brief. Maybe a weekend with Cecily with help and I'd say Jeremy will be there also.'

Frankie laughed. 'He's a great kid. Just like Rose was at that age.'

Simon turned to her and smiled. 'Let's not talk any more about Amy. This weekend is about us.'

The night away had been everything she had hoped it would be. The resort was quiet with only a few guests staying through the tropical months. March was not a popular tourist time and the weather was too hot for most, who waited until the cooler months when they could swim in the ocean and sit on the beach during the day.

This was what the days and nights had been like when she had first met Simon. Romantic, exciting and everything organised for perfect meals and a relaxing time. For the first time in a long while she enjoyed the luxury of a restaurant meal and icy cool cocktails. The food and drinks were brought to their cabin and they sat on the verandah, looking over the ocean towards Bowen as the sun sank lower in the sky.

The ocean sparkled in the afternoon sun and a few sailing boats skimmed across the waves further out. Heavy sultry clouds hung low and as the sun dipped below them and then the horizon, spectacular reds and oranges splashed across the sky. The resort was situated on the northern end of a bay and faced west, giving the added bonus of the sun setting over the ocean.

They'd talked for hours, laughing as they reminisced about their first dates, the bulky silhouette of Gloucester Island to the north reminding Frankie of when Simon had rescued her from a boating outing with his brother. 'I was so seasick and had vomit all over me. It's a wonder you didn't tip me out of the boat before we landed.'

He chuckled. 'Didn't you notice I kept my distance until you washed yourself when you swam.' He reached over and pulled her towards him. 'I'd hoped you'd swim naked that day, but you kept your clothes on.'

Frankie kissed him, her hands wrapping around his shoulders. 'You've never told me that. I thought you were such a gentleman at the time.'

His hands moved over her bare legs. 'You should have known better.'

She pressed against him, a familiar ache in her body as he kissed up and down her neck. Holding her tight he whispered in her ear. 'I'm not sure this is a good place for me to make love to you.'

She laughed as she pulled away and stood up, holding his hand in hers. 'It's not.'

Simon picked her up gently, her arms wrapped around his neck as he carried her into the cabin, the door closing firmly behind them.

* * *

The weekend was rejuvenating for both of them. A long walk in the late afternoon, followed by food, wine, and swims in the pool, was a perfect way to unwind and sleeping in after a full night's slumber was the icing on the cake.

Frankie was revitalised, her body relaxed, her mind clear from worry. 'You look like a different person,' Simon commented as they prepared to leave.

'I feel great. It's so nice to spend time together, just the two of us. On one hand I can't wait to get home to see Charlotte but then ...'

He kissed her softly, finishing her sentence. 'There's Amy. I feel the same. I could stay here for days and just make love to you.'

She laughed. 'Is that all you think of?'

He pinched her on the bottom. 'When you're in those tiny shorts. Yes.'

CHAPTER 13

The weekend had also put a spring back in Simon's step and not only did he make sure that each night he spent some time alone with Frankie with no interruptions, but he also became stricter with Amy.

'Frankie and I need some time together. After dinner and when Charlotte's asleep, we're going to sit down on the beach without any disruptions.'

'Whatever.'

'You'll be responsible for Charlotte and if she wakes up you can come and get us.'

'I'm not your babysitter.'

'No, you're not. You're my daughter and you're also Charlotte's sister, and you will make sure that you sit in the lounge and listen for her in case she wakes. Not in your room with your headphones on.'

'Whatever.'

Simon's patience was wearing thin. 'If you can't do that for us, then ...' he hesitated.

'What,' Amy said, a sneer on her face.

'Forget about Frankie or me, driving you to Jeremy's or anywhere else you want to go. You can just hang out here.'

'You can't do that. This place is so far away from everything I can't go anywhere unless you drive me. There's not even a bus I can catch. You can't make me a prisoner in my own home. Sometimes it's like being in jail living here.'

So dramatic he thought as he spoke slowly to make sure she understood. 'So, do you agree that you will sit in the lounge and listen for Charlotte? If she's not asleep you could pat her or read her a book. I've seen Jeremy do that, surely you could too.' He looked hard at his daughter, her sullen eyes downcast, the ridiculous black beanie pulled low on her forehead. It was like they went one step forward with her and then three backward. 'I'm talking to you. Give me your assurance that we can trust you to do that. We'll just be down the front on the beach.'

'Whatever.'

'Is that a, yes?'

'Yep.'

* * *

The evening hour, or sometimes a bit longer together, became routine and Frankie relished the time alone with Simon. It was a chance to catch up on the day-to-day events and plan for the weeks ahead. Some nights they'd sit quietly, their eyes cast to the sky, following a satellite tracking across the expanse or watching a falling star as it plunged through the inky darkness. Other times she would sit on the sand between his knees, his arms wrapped around her as she leaned back into his chest. As they watched the clouds race across the sky and the moon throw its rays across the ocean she felt like she was a million miles from anywhere.

One night the sky had been clear, the moon lighting up the beach and the ocean as if it was daylight. 'It's perfect.' She'd whispered, Simon's kisses sending goosebumps tingling over her arms and legs.

'You're perfect,' he replied, his arms wrapped around her, their bodies close to each other.

* * *

Later that month a tropical low formed in the Coral Sea. Frankie noticed the change in everyone. People seemed to walk faster at the shops, stocking up on supplies, the usual slow stroll transformed into a quicker pace. The locals talked about the rain that might come their way, what precautions they'd put in place and where the low, if it turned into a cyclone might cross the coast.

She felt a bit on edge. Everyone she talked to treated it like it was just a bit of rain coming and it was almost as if they were excited rather than apprehensive about it. Artie and Maureen called over one afternoon. They'd brought a bag of mangoes with them and she made them a cup of tea, sitting on the verandah together. She'd tried to get Amy to come out and join them but she'd only thrown Frankie a surly look before returning to her guitar. It was all she seemed to do these days, strum and sing, strum and sing. Jeremy had lent her the guitar; at least it kept her occupied. Frankie was confused how someone who appreciated something as cultural as music could be such an unhappy, nasty person.

'Amy not joining us?' Maureen asked, looking around to see if she was about to appear.

'No, she's not. I asked her but she declined.'

Artie grinned, holding his hand out for Charlotte to play with. 'You're not going to be like that are you?' he said. He was rewarded with a smile and she held out her arms for Artie to take her. He bounced her on his lap, Maureen making noises and clapping her hands to get the baby's attention.

'Are you all ready if there's a big blow?' Artie asked her.

'That's where Simon is at the moment,' she replied. 'Cecily's husband is away at the mines and she wanted some big branches cut down and taken away. There were a few bits of tin and other rubbish he was going to collect in his ute and take to the dump. He'll do that and then he has some things to put away here.'

'I reckon it's going to come our way. We're due for one,' Maureen said.

'Do you think we're safe in these houses?' Frankie looked around, the thought of strong winds and high seas made her nervous.

'Our house has stood for over a hundred years and yours is the same. They'll keep standing. Simon will know the safest area in the house to take shelter if it gets too bad.' Artie passed Charlotte to Maureen so he could drink his cup of tea. 'He leaned back in his chair and crossed his bare feet. 'Probably won't come to much. Often it's a lot of hype and then they just bring a lot of rain and wind or they go in the other direction. Bit like a woman, you know, they can't make their mind up.'

He put his cup down on the table, chuckling as Maureen growled at him. 'Watch what you say, Artie. You're outnumbered here.'

He sipped his tea, his eyes twinkling as he looked at Frankie. 'I'm always outnumbered. Story of my life.'

'Oh, your poor thing,' Maureen chortled, 'So hard done by.'

Frankie watched the two of them as they hopped in Artie's ute and drove away. They'd been married for over fifty years and no doubt with five daughters, husbands, grandkids and even great grandkids, they'd had their share of ups and downs. 'Wouldn't change a thing,' Maureen had once told her. 'Family is everything. Family and health.'

She thought about that now as Amy came out through the front door, slamming it hard behind her. 'I'm not going to school tomorrow. They say if it rains the roads will get cut.'

Frankie turned around, Charlotte who was in her arms, smiled and made cute baby noises when she saw Amy. 'There isn't even any rain here yet. Artie said it could go in the other direction. Let's just wait and see.'

Amy turned on her heels and stomped back inside. Frankie shut her eyes, hoping that Amy would disappear. When did kids usually leave home and get their own place? She jiggled Charlotte, laughing as her chubby little fingers grabbed her face, her lips pressing over Frankie's face. 'Kisses for Mum,' she said, hugging her tight. Thank goodness for Charlotte and Simon. At least the three of them were a tight-knit family. She looked for Simon's ute, hoping he'd be home soon. The last thing she wanted was to go inside and face another one of Amy's tirades by herself. A walk down to the water would fill in time until he came home.

CHAPTER 14

*A*lthough the sky was clear, with only a string of dark clouds on the horizon, the water threw up a different colour than usual. She stared at it, trying to work out what had changed. The surface was littered with small waves and a murky tone washed across the water instead of the usual clear one. The air was still though, not even a breeze, and her mind was put at ease as she watched seagulls diving in and out of the water, their calls echoing across the beach. Perhaps it wasn't going to be that bad. After all there wasn't even any wind at the moment.

She looked up at the palm trees, their leaves motionless, not even the slightest movement in the air. Charlotte squirmed in her arms and she put her down, letting her wriggle her toes in the sand. She squealed with delight, her hands grabbing handfuls of sand before attempting to put it in her mouth. Frankie pulled her hands away, diverting her attention with a coconut that lay next to her. Charlotte rolled it like a ball, picking it up and throwing it back down.

Frankie peered across the water towards the horizon. There was a cluster of dark, bruised clouds hanging low their ominous presence stretching across the eastern reaches. Surely there would be stronger winds than this if the cyclone was going to cross the coast anywhere near them. She sighed heavily as she picked Charlotte up and brushed the sand from her legs and arms. . Time to face angry Amy, she thought. Perhaps a cyclone wouldn't be too bad compared to her.

Over the next three days the winds strengthened and the sky went from its usual clear blue to a murky grey colour. Artie and Simon worked together to make sure the live-stock were taken care of and there was nothing loose lying around. They helped each other board up windows and tie down anything that couldn't be put under cover. Both had timber panels in their sheds that fitted into slots that were fixed on the outside of the windows.

'Don't look so worried, love,' Artie assured her. 'We've been through this all before. It's just part of living here.'

On the afternoon of the 27th of March, Simon, Frankie, and Amy stood on the beach, looking out at the huge dark mass of clouds that loomed on the horizon. The sky above them was grey and dark and spits of rain dotted the beach. Simon held Charlotte close, her head tucked into him to avoid the wind. The sand flew up as gusts kicked across the beach and even Amy was mesmerised by the changes over the last couple of hours. Schools had been closed so she was happy for once to be home. 'Do you think we'll get it bad here?' she asked Simon.

'It's not that far from us now. It's a category three at the moment but that will change once it gets closer to the coast. The updated forecast says it's supposed to cross the coast in another day or so. You never know though, they swing around a bit. It could end up anywhere.'

'Cyclone Debbie,' Amy said. 'Cool. Can't wait.'

Frankie's stomach started to churn, like butterflies bouncing around inside. 'I don't see anything, cool, about it.' She looked at Simon. 'I didn't sign up for this. I don't like storms, never mind cyclones.'

Amy obviously picked up on her fear. 'Have you ever seen The Wizard of Oz. It'll be just like that. Suck the house up, spin it around and throw it into the heavens. Cool.'

Simon put his arm around Frankie. 'We're used to cyclones up here. I've been through plenty. You just have to sit them out. Wait until they've passed and then you clean up. I've put in a lot of extra strengthening for the house and the new shed. I'm confident that we'll be okay here. If I wasn't I'd get you to go into the evacuation centres in town, but we're safe here.' He stared out across the ocean. 'I don't like the way that ocean's kicking up though or the colour of it. I reckon we're in for a big one.'

She shivered. 'I would have thought Artie and Maureen would have gone into the cyclone shelter in Proserpine.'

'There's no way they'll budge,' he said. 'Their kids want them to go and stay at one of their places until it passes but they'll want to stay with the house. We all have a safe area. Their downstairs bathroom is Besser block. It's big like a bunker. They'll have it all set up and supplies in there ready. As long as Artie has his beer in there he'll be okay.'

Amy skipped back up to the house in front of them. 'She's really getting on my nerves,' Frankie said. 'Seriously, she is constantly antagonising me, I know she's trying to stir me up about this cyclone and she constantly ignores Charlotte.'

Simon passed Charlotte back to her. 'Yeah, I'm getting ready for a big argument with her. She's pushing me to the edge at the moment also. Let's just get through these next few days and then we'll tackle her head-on together.'

Frankie cuddled up to him as he wrapped his arms around her. He hugged her and Charlotte. 'You're really about to become a north Queenslander now. If this one crosses where it looks like it should, it will be right over the top of us. You'll get to know what our storms are like.'

Frankie pulled a silly face and pushed her hair so it hung messily around her face. 'Cool. Just cool.'

'Well done,' Simon chuckled, 'Now all you need is a black beanie.'

CHAPTER 15

During the night the wind picked up and sticks and branches hitting the roof kept Frankie awake. She got up several times to check on Charlotte, eventually bringing her back into bed with her. Simon was also restless and had gone outside a couple of times to check on the weather. 'The winds picking up out there. Debbie's coming,' he whispered as he snuggled into Charlotte, her chubby arm thrown across his face as she slept. 'I looked in on Amy,' he added. 'She's happy.' Both dogs had been allowed to come inside and were snuggled up on the mat in her bedroom, her eyes shut and sleeping like a baby when he checked.

* * *

In the morning they turned the lights on, the dark clouds making it more like night than day. The wind howled outside and Simon continually checked that everything was in place. 'I don't think the power will last much longer,' he said. 'Don't look so worried Frankie. We'll be okay.' Simon watched his phone for updates. 'It's still a while off. We just need to sit it out.'

Frankie hadn't let go of Charlotte since they'd got up and hung onto her now even as she slept in her arms. 'I can't believe the noise. It's so loud. Surely it can't get any worse than this.'

'This is just the start of it. It will get a lot stronger, so be prepared for the noise.'

'Are you sure we'll be alright here?'

'When it does get really bad we'll go into the bathroom. That room is made of Besser block and has been built like a bunker. Everything we need is in there. I've made sure we're well prepared.' He put his arm around her shoulders. 'We've done everything we can, now stop looking so scared.'

It was hard to believe that it could get any worse and she took deep breaths as rain lashed against the windows. The house shook on its stumps when stronger gusts swept across them and a couple of smaller trees blew over, their roots sticking up in the air. A sick feeling in her stomach niggled when she thought of what it would be like at night when you wouldn't be able to see what was happening or when the power went off. Simon said their phones wouldn't work either once it hit but he had a satellite phone plus a radio to check on what was happening. 'Once it's here we just need to stay where we are,' he told her. 'Everyone's in the same situation and the emergency services won't budge, they'll stay in the shelter from when it hits until it's passed over. No one can be outside until we get the all-clear.'

Her nerves were on edge and she'd yelled at Amy

when she'd got up and let the dogs out. 'What the hell are you doing? Shut the door.'

Amy had turned and thrown her one of her dirtiest looks. 'They need to pee, you idiot. Calm down. You're a mother, aren't you supposed to stay calm.' She smirked at Frankie. 'You can tell you're a city person.'

Frankie gritted her teeth and turned her back. Why did Amy always find the opportune moment when Simon wasn't around to be her rudest? She couldn't be bothered putting her in her place. There were bigger things to worry about.

Simon came back in, the wind howling outside as he shut the door. Both dogs were right behind him, their tails wagging as they roamed through the house. 'Amy, get them settled in the bathroom. Put down some old towels for them. They'll have to stay in there with us once this hits.'

Frankie's voice was a squeak. 'You mean it's not here yet? Isn't it hitting now?'

'It's supposed to cross about midnight tonight. You've got about another fourteen hours or so of this yet. And that's just until it gets here. Let's hope it crosses quickly and blows itself out once it hits the coast.'

Simon had talked her into putting Charlotte down in the cot which they'd dragged into the lounge room. She didn't seem bothered by the noise and snuggled down under her blankets. 'The darkness is making her sleep more,' Frankie said.

'C'mon and I'll make you a cup of tea.' He put his arm around her shoulders. At least the dogs are keeping Amy company. Keeps her from annoying us.'

Frankie sat down, her pounding heart settling a little

as she sipped a cup of tea. Every now and again the house shook, the noise from outside, deafening, as the gales strengthened. Simon kept the radio on, the news updating continually as everyone from Townsville to Mackay waited to see where the cyclone would cross.

'Where are they saying?' she asked, after coming back from checking Charlotte.

Simon didn't answer straight away. She glared at him. 'Where?'

'Um, they think Dingo Beach, Airlie Beach.'

'That's us.'

'Pretty much.'

She was still glaring at him when his phone rang.

It was Maureen, and Frankie could hear her voice even over the sound of the wind. 'Artie's had a fall. I know it's terrible outside but he's in a bad way and I can't get him into the car and I can't get onto anyone to help. I've tried to ring the two daughters that live the closest but I'd say their phones are already out. The ambulance answered their phones though and they say if we can get him to the highway they'll come and get him. We'll have to be quick though because they'll go into lockdown in an hour or so. They think it's going to cross right over us.'

'What's he done,' Simon said.

'Silly old bugger. He tried to get up on the ladder and secure a loose piece of tin that he'd missed. He slipped, hadn't even been drinking. Poor old thing. He's in a fair bit of pain. I'd say he's broken something. Maybe his ankle. It doesn't look good, I'm telling you. Artie's tough, but this is stretching his pain threshold.'

Frankie could hear Artie in the background. 'Tell 'em they'll be right to come and get me, but we'll need both of them. You can't lift me, Maureen. That cyclone's a while out yet. We've got time. I don't want to be stuck in here for days with a broken leg. There's a window of time to get me out and for Simon to get back.'

Frankie held her breath. How the hell could she take Charlotte out in this?

Simon was already putting his rain jacket on. 'We're coming Maureen. We'll be there in five minutes. Make sure you have your overnight bags ready.

CHAPTER 16

'*I* can't take Charlotte out in this,' Frankie knew her voice sounded frantic but the sound of the wind from outside was getting to her. A roaring noise that came from the beach had also increased. 'Is that the sound of the waves? It's nearly here.'

Simon grabbed her by the shoulders. 'You aren't going to take Charlotte. Maureen needs both of us, otherwise, she wouldn't have asked. She's been through these cyclones before and it must be bad for her to ask us both to come over. We've got a few hours yet until this gets really bad.'

'What? How can it get worse than this?'

'Believe me it will.' He disappeared, coming back with Amy behind him.

This time he grabbed her by the shoulders. 'Listen carefully to me. Frankie and I need to go and help Maureen. Artie's broken his leg and they need us to drive them out onto the main road. Frankie can drive so I'll have to take her and not you.'

Amy scrunched her face up. 'There's no way I'm going anywhere in this. Are you mad?'

'They need our help. We should have a couple of hours up our sleeve. We need you to look after Charlotte. She's asleep at the moment.'

Frankie pulled her raincoat on. 'If she wakes up there's a bottle in the fridge and more in the esky with the other food. Nurse her and sit in the bathroom with the dogs.' She looked Amy in the eye. 'I've done lots for you over the past months and now I'm trusting you to look after her. You know what to do.'

Amy chewed on gum, her arms folded. 'Hope she stays asleep. How long will you be?'

'We should only be a couple of hours,' Simon said. 'Keep your phone with you and remember that bathroom is the safe place to be if it gets any worse. Take Charlotte and the dogs in there with you if you need to.'

Frankie took one last look at the sleeping Charlotte. Hopefully they'd be back before she woke up. She gave Amy one last look and gritted her teeth. 'Look after her, please.'

Once they were off the verandah the weather was a lot worse than Frankie had imagined. She lowered her head and hung onto the back of Simon's coat as they made their way to the shed. The wind sounded like a train, the noise so loud that she couldn't hear if the car had started or not. In the background the pounding of the waves on the beach thundered, the squalls pushing against the palm trees and other trees that were bent over with the force.

Small sticks and twigs blew against the side of the car as she drove out through the driveway and onto the track that would lead to next door.

Maureen was waiting at the door, her usual cheery face, worried and drawn. 'Jees, Artie can usually handle anything but this is really pushing him. They hurried into the loungeroom where Artie lay, his face white, his leg in a splint that Maureen had made from two broomsticks. He attempted a smile. 'I've had a bit of self-medication. A nip of brandy. I need more than that though.'

Maureen hurried back and forth, making sure she had everything she needed. 'We're so sorry to get you out in this but we didn't know what else to do. The ambulance is out on other jobs. Someone's had a heart attack at Bloomfield and there's a car stuck in floodwaters out the back here somewhere. I've just been in contact with them though and we'll meet them in half an hour on the highway and then you can get back to the baby and Amy. We just have to get poor old Artie into the car.'

Artie tried to grin but his face clenched up and he closed his eyes. He held Maureen's hand as Simon and Frankie got either side of him and helped him to the car. They stopped a couple of times when the pain got too much, giving him some time to get his breath and keep going. The wind had picked up even in the short time they'd been in the house. Frankie kept checking her time, praying that Charlotte stayed asleep.

'I knew you had Amy to look after the baby. We should get there quickly and then you need to get back. The roads are closed due to flooding on the other side of town and there's only one way in and out at the moment.' Maureen ran to the car and opened the door, throwing her bag inside. 'C'mon Artie, we're nearly there,' she encouraged him, helping to guide him into the back seat.

Frankie was about to drive off when she remembered the dog. 'Where's Riley?'

'Oh my goodness,' Maureen said. 'He's locked in the garage.'

Simon got out and ran, the wind howling as they waited in the car for him to return. They couldn't see for the rain and Frankie hoped he'd find the dog quickly. It didn't take long for him to return and she jumped as the car door flung open. 'C'mon Riley,' Maureen said, guiding the large dog to a sitting position at her feet. 'You'll have to take him back with you,' she said to Frankie, who was waiting for Simon to get back in with Artie. 'We can't take him and there's no way we'll get him to the daughter's house. They'll be cut off.'

'We'll look after him, Maureen,' Simon said. 'Don't worry about him, we'll take him back and he can be inside with our dogs. They're in the laundry next to us. We'll make sure he's okay.'

Frankie drove while Simon sat with Artie trying to keep his leg still. Simon made a joke about calamities happening in the back seats of cars which did make everyone smile, and there was even a funny quip from Artie about babies arriving.

'Maureen had one of our girls in the middle of a cyclone,' he said. 'The hospital lost power and the doc waded through a creek to get there. Gotta take our hats off to you women.' He flinched as Frankie hit a pothole and she slowed down, watching the water creeping over the edges of the road. At least there wasn't anyone else out driving. No one would be stupid enough to be out in this weather.

It was hard to see through the windscreen, the rain pelting down was horizontal and the wind picked up anything in its path. Trees bent over with the force of the wind and small creeks were starting to spill over the road. When she turned onto the highway it was even harder to see and Simon talked to her, guiding her into a small dirt area well off to the side of the road where they'd arranged to meet the ambulance. 'They've already picked someone else up but they said they'll fit us both in,' Maureen said.

'Would it be quicker for us to drive you into the hospital,' Frankie asked, worried about how long they'd have to wait.

Artie piped up from the back seat. 'You won't get back if you do that. Those creeks will get up quickly on the highway.'

They talked for a bit longer, the car moving and swaying with each gust of wind. A picture on a billboard that had been flapping wildly on the other side of the road started to peel off, a huge photo of an idyllic beach with blue sky and lush palm trees ripping in half and rising up into the air. Another gust took it flying over the top of them, thankfully clearing the car and landing in the cane fields next to them. Frankie's stomach turned as she looked out through the window. The gullies in the fields were quickly filling with water, the cane that usually stood tall, bending and in some places flattened with the wind and rain.

She looked in the rear-view mirror and through the back windscreen. A large tree flew through the air behind them, landing on the other side of the road. Thank goodness she thought, as she gained a glimpse of flashing lights coming towards them. 'I see the ambulance. They're coming.'

Before long an ambulance was parked beside them, the two paramedics moving quickly as they slid Artie onto a stretcher before getting him into the safety of the ambulance. Frankie hopped out of the car and popped her head in the back, pleased to see that there was somewhere for Maureen to sit. Artie lifted his hand and she put hers in it. He gave a gentle squeeze, his face relieved as he looked at her. 'Thanks, mate,' he said. 'Now get back home to those two girls.'

CHAPTER 17

*I*t was a relief for Frankie to sit in the passenger's seat rather than drive and Simon passed her a towel to dry herself with. She peered through the windscreen at the driving rain, thankful to be headed in the direction of home. Riley had jumped in the back and stared out through the back windscreen, no doubt wondering what was going on and why he was not with his owners. The wind seemed to have changed direction, swirling one way and then the other. It was a relief when she spotted the sign to Dingo Beach through the driving rain and they slowly turned off the highway.

Simon clenched the steering wheel, the window wipers moving rapidly against the flood of water that flung against the glass. 'It's getting pretty wild out there. I'll be pleased when we're off these roads. It's hard to see.'

She got out her phone. 'I'll just ring Amy and let her know we're on the way back.'

She looked at the screen of her phone. There was no

reception. 'The phone's got no signal.' She grabbed Simon's but it was the same.

'I'd say maybe the towers aren't working. There will be lines starting to come down. The last report said that the cyclone will cross late tonight. It's about lockdown time.'

'Can you drive quicker?'

'I have to be careful. It will be okay. don't look so worried.'

Ripples of panic ran through her body and she felt like bursting into tears. Her hands clenched the seat belt and she willed him to drive quicker. The clouds had sunk lower and the mountains were no longer visible. Although it was only early in the afternoon the light had faded and it seemed more like night-time. Simon turned off the road onto the track that would lead them through the scrub and out to the cane fields. From there it should be a quick and easy run home.

The car headlights shone on the road that was littered with branches and sticks. 'Shit,' Simon yelled, slamming on his brakes. She grabbed the dashboard to stop herself from lurching forward. In front of them, blocking their way, was a large gum tree. Its thick trunk straddled the road, its massive head of branches flattening the vegetation where it had fallen.

Frankie's hands and legs started to shake. 'How do we get around that?'

The bush around them was bent over and other large branches were breaking off and flying through the air. Simon turned to her. 'If we turn around and try and go back around the other way it will take ages and I wouldn't be surprised if there are power lines down. That's why I came this way. There's no way around that tree and it's dangerous to sit here in the car with all these big trees around. There's no one to ring for help. Emergency services won't come out now.'

She sat upright and grabbed her phone. 'We have to get home. What if we run from here?'

She could tell he was working out the time it would take. 'I reckon we're about a half-hour walk from home. It's bloody dangerous out there but we don't have a choice. We can't stay here.' He undid his seat belt. 'Are you up to it because we don't have a choice?' He leaned back and grabbed the rope he'd attached to Riley. 'Sorry mate, you don't either. You're coming with us.'

Simon grabbed her hand as they stood in front of the car. They stepped over the tree, looking back at the car that was already starting to get covered in branches and twigs. The wind howled savagely and it was difficult to walk, never mind run. In front of them the dirt track was barely visible. If only the light would hold out a bit so they could see where they were going. Simon held Riley tightly. He looked at Frankie and squeezed her hand. 'Slow jog, c'mon we can do it.'

Her throat tightened and she pushed back her rising terror as branches flew through the air. Sheets of rain pushed in front of them but she held tight to Simon's hand. They needed to get back to Charlotte and Amy.

CHAPTER 18

rankie's legs throbbed and her chest ached. The wind had swung around again and now it was pushing against them, making even walking nearly impossible. The noises were deafening and the roar of the wind intensified. Simon's arm wrapped around her shoulder and he yelled in her ear. 'There's the gate. We're here.' He dragged her along, her feet struggling to wade through the mud and debris, her head down as the rain pelted across her face. It had taken a bit longer than what they'd thought it would, the wind and rain working against them every step of the way. The sound of metal tearing made both of them look up and they watched as half of the old shed peeled away and flew through the air, sheets of tin landing in the paddocks next to it.

Simon clung to her arm and dragged her forward, helping her to step around and over the trees and branches scattered across the yard. She tried to look around at the carnage but the yard was already unrecognisable, the contents of the old shed and shredded foliage covering the ground, her gardens and lawn unrecognisable. Grasping the stair rails she pulled herself up onto the verandah. Simon opened the front door and pushed her inside, Riley and him following, the sound of the door slamming behind them barely audible above the din of the wind.

When Simon grabbed her arms and shook her she tried to talk but nothing came out. He pushed her hair back from her face and tried to take her useless rain jacket coat off, but she was shaking so badly that nothing seemed to go the way it was supposed to.

'Where have you both been,' Amy's voice was shrill and Frankie looked up to see her bouncing Charlotte on her hip, a torch in her hand. 'I was scared to death. The power went off not long after you left and the phone isn't working. I was terrified but I tried not to show Charlie that.' She squeezed the baby to her, Charlotte gurgling and smiling as if nothing was wrong.

Bursting into tears, Frankie held her arms out to Charlotte, but Amy backed away from her. 'Look at you, you're drenched. Get out of your clothes first. She's okay I've got her. You're a mess and you're shaking. I'll sit in the bathroom with her while you get changed.'

Simon managed to get out of his wet clothes first and quickly got towels and clean clothes for Frankie. He helped her get changed and dried her hair, rubbing her arms and talking to her. Eventually she started to breathe evenly but her nerves were still on edge. The noise outside seemed to be getting louder, heavy thuds and bangs on the roof making her jump every time.

Simon went and got Charlotte from Amy. 'Get those

dogs into the laundry. They'll be safe in there and it will leave us more room.'

Amy moved quickly. 'I'll put towels down and some water for them. I won't feed them because our two will fight with Riley.'

'Good idea,' Simon said. 'They don't need food yet anyway. It won't hurt them.'

By the time Amy came back into the lounge Frankie had started to feel a bit better. A couple of camping lamps threw some light around the room and Charlotte looked happy in Simon's arms. Thank goodness she was too little to realise what the noise was. When Amy passed her a large cup of hot tea that she'd made on the gas cooker, Frankie once again burst into tears. She blubbered like a kid. 'I was so scared. A tree fell. I was worried about you both here without us. What if we hadn't been able to get back.'

Amy came and sat beside her, offering her a biscuit. 'I was fine here. I was worried about you two out there in this crazy wind. I've been listening to the radio. They say it's going to cross late tonight. This isn't even the worst of it yet.'

Simon sat down on the floor in front of them, the room eerie in the dim light. 'It just hasn't let up. It's time we move into the bathroom. The mattresses are in there and we've got blankets and whatever else we need. We're ready for the night. I'll just move some of the furniture further away from the windows in the bedrooms. I'm not sure if those boards we put up are going to hold out too much longer in this.'

Frankie went to stand up. She'd finished her tea and passed her cup to Simon. 'Sit down,' Amy said. 'Dad and I can do this. Your face is really white. You look after Charlie and we'll get everything else sorted. She must be due a feed.'

Frankie did as she was told, her heart thumping hard as the noise continued from outside. What would happen to all the animals that were outside. Luckily they had the dogs inside, and bunkered down for the night in the laundry. She gazed down at Charlotte, contently feeding and looking up every so often and smiling at her. Thank goodness they had made it back. Now all they had to do was hope the house held together and that the cyclone passed over quickly. Surely it would blow itself out once it did.

CHAPTER 19

*T*he bathroom was definitely the most secure place in the house and Simon had made sure they had everything they needed well in advance. The only light came from a small camping light. They'd use that and preserve the other lights for what was to come. 'We'll be without power for a long while after this,' Simon said, taking Charlotte from Frankie. 'We have the generators on standby but going by what we saw outside before, the damage from this will be huge.'

Outside the room it was pitch dark, with not a scrap of light coming from anywhere. The noise outside was horrendous, sounding like a freight train was driving in through the lounge room. Some windows had blown out on the northern side of the house and Simon and Amy had moved everything out of those rooms into the lounge. As they shut the bathroom door and huddled together Frankie felt like the world was coming to an end. Her face must have revealed how she was feeling because Amy linked her arm through hers, their backs propped up against pillows that leaned against the bathtub. 'It's okay, Frankie. We'll be safe. Dad's been through these cyclones lots of times and he won't let anything happen to us. Look, Charlie's asleep.'

Frankie looked through the dim light and Charlotte's eyes were closed, her body covered by Simon's jacket as he held her. Simon looked up at them. 'It's safe in here. There's no need to worry. Everything else might go, but this section and the laundry will be okay.'

No one slept much that night. Frankie dozed on and off, the three of them lying next to each other on the mattresses that lined the floor, Charlotte snuggled between them. When Amy came back from a toilet visit she pushed Frankie with her hands, gesturing for her to move next to Simon. 'Get in the middle, you'll feel safer.'

Frankie did as she was told, her hand reaching up to hold Charlotte's who was still fast asleep. Simon kissed the top of her head and whispered. 'It's still got a while to go. It doesn't seem to be moving very fast. They usually pass over a bit quicker than this. Try and get some sleep.'

In the morning when she sat up she felt like the noise had increased and she could hear tin and timber banging from the other side of the house. They ate some of the food they'd brought into the bathroom, a cup of tea that Amy made tasting like the best drink in the world. The young girl had set up a space just outside in the hallway where she had a small gas cooker and everything needed to get food ready. She had also organised the dog food and cleaned up their mess from the night before. Thankfully the toilet was next to the bathroom so they had everything they needed close by in the small, protected part of the house.

When Amy came and sat down she passed a toy to Charlotte. 'The baby room is a mess. Half the roof's gone and the water is pouring in. I've stacked some of her things in the laundry to try and save them.'

'There's nothing we can do,' Simon said. 'This cyclone is different than the ones I've been through before. It has blown for a long while. They don't usually last this long.' Just as he spoke a calm descended on the house. The wind stopped and the rain eased before it also could no longer be heard.

Simon stood up and looked at his watch. 'It's one a.m. This calm will be the eye. Don't think for one second it's over. It will be quiet for a couple of hours and then we'll get the back end of the storm. Stay here and I'll check the damage so far. I don't want anyone going outside. There'll be power lines and all sorts of debris out there. We just need to stay put.'

Eventually he'd let Amy and Frankie come out onto the verandah to have a look around. It appeared that half the house had been blown off, bits of timber and tin hanging loose and the windows gone from the northern side of the building. When Simon shone his torch around they could see that the yard was covered in trees and foliage, half of the shed also lying in amongst the rubble. They let the dogs have a quick run around before calling them back inside. She watched Simon who was looking further down towards the beach, the waves churning violently against the sand, much further than usual.

Palm trees left standing started to sway again as the wind picked up and some fibro wall panels tumbled across the yard as strong gusts pushed from the other direction.

'It's the second half coming.' He whistled to the dogs who flew up the stairs and back into the laundry. Amy followed them and made sure they had food and water before locking them in. For the first time she looked nervous. 'Will this second half be as bad, Dad?' she asked.

He ushered them into the bathroom. 'I hate to say it but it's possible it could be worse.'

Cyclone Debbie hovered above them for the next day. The wind and rain intensified and the house shook and swayed on its foundations as the destructive storm continued on its path. At one stage it sounded like the roof was lifting and the bathroom door shook loudly. Charlotte was starting to get cranky. She was sick of being in the one spot for so long. Frankie tried to feed her again but she screamed and threw herself down on the mattress. Clearly she had had enough.

Simon got up every so often and tried to look out through the door. He'd shut the doors to the two bedrooms where the roof had blown away and the loungeroom floor was layered with towels and sheets to try and soak up the water that gushed under the doors. 'It's moving slowly. I've never been in one that went for so many hours with such strength. I just need that roof to hold until it's over.'

Amy took Charlotte from her. She laid down on her back and put Charlotte on her tummy, bouncing her up and down and clapping her hands. When she started singing, Charlotte stopped crying and jumped up and down, her baby giggles drawing their attention for a moment. They laughed as she banged down hard on Amy's stomach. Amy sang some more songs and for a while they forgot about the noise outside. 'She's so cute,'

Amy said as she stopped to get her breath. 'She loves me.'

Frankie smiled. 'She does. At the moment she wants you more than your dad or me. I guess that's what happens when you're all stuck in a tiny space for two days and nights.'

* * *

The winds and rain continued through the day and that night. The next morning. Frankie woke to Charlotte sitting on her, her little hands grabbing at her face. 'I've changed her nappy,' Amy said, 'and she's had a bottle. Dad said to let you sleep.'

Frankie sat up. 'Where is he?'

'He's outside. It looks like the worst is over. It's still pouring rain and the wind is blowing but nothing like the last two days. We've let the dogs out. You want to see it out there. It's like a bomb has gone off.'

* * *

Eventually the cyclone passed over the coastline and moved inland. It left behind a path of destruction with torrential rain and damaging winds felt from the islands not far off the coast to the central area west of Mackay. When it tracked further south-east it left behind more damage with high winds and catastrophic flooding experienced from Brisbane down to the northern areas of New South Wales.

They listened to its progress on the radio. 'I can't believe it's damaged so much up here,' Frankie said, 'and now people down south have also lost their homes and businesses from the same storm.'

'They reckon it sat over us and only moved about seven kilometres an hour. No wonder it felt like it was never going to go,' Amy added in.

* * *

The next couple of days were spent cleaning up what they could. Frankie and Amy concentrated on the inside, moving items to one side that could be salvaged and throwing anything that couldn't, onto a pile near the front steps that was getting bigger by the hour. Simon's chainsaw went non-stop and after a while he had cleared a pathway from the house to the sheds and down to the beach. Past the gate there was no way of going or coming, the entire area littered with large trees and debris. Simon's cane was flattened, the area inaccessible with water spilling over the creeks and tracks, his dams unrecognisable with tin and trees floating on their surface. Plasterboard was strewn across the driveway, and fences were flattened leaving livestock roaming freely. Some of Artie's cattle and horses stood in the paddock over further, unable to go anywhere due to the trees that surrounded them.

Thankfully a generator supplied them with electricity but the phones were out and they'd had no communication with anyone.

'That plasterboard down the yard there looks like it's come from Artie's walls,' Simon said. 'Who knows what's left of their place? Hopefully it's fared better than ours. At least they weren't there.'

***

The following day the three of them stood in a cleared section of the front yard, looking back at the house. A third of the roof had gone and two bedrooms were bare, their walls and floors exposed as light rain continued to fall.

Simon ran his hand through his hair. It wasn't just the worry of the house and sheds to repair, there was also the loss of crops and livestock to tally up. At this stage he wasn't really sure what was left standing. 'We're lucky we've only lost those two rooms and the old shed', he said. 'The main shed is fairly new and cyclone proof so it hasn't suffered so badly. The equipment in there is okay.' They'd walked down to the beach, a narrow path that Simon had cleared letting them make their way through the debris. The ocean was a dark brown murky slosh with trees and branches floating on its surface, the beach littered with debris. Coconut trees stood headless, their battered trunks the only part left standing. Further up the beach a couple of huge fig trees lay on their sides, their massive branches sprawled across the ground, their roots in the air.

The next day a helicopter landed on the beach. It was the first contact they'd had since the cyclone began and they'd hugged the two men who jumped out to greet them. In the following days, crews from different rescue groups managed to get to them and start the clean-up. Before long they had access to their road in and out. Simon had walked out with another worker, cutting their way through the wreckage, back to where they had left the car the night they'd taken Artie in. Their chainsaws soon cleared the large tree that had stopped them from driving all the way home. Dents and scratches covered the car but it was driveable and at least in working order.

Even though they were able to make their way along some of their tracks, the roads further out were still inaccessible so for now they made use of the supplies the volunteers brought with them.

Once the power was restored. Frankie was kept busy ringing the insurance company and talking to her family who had been worried when they couldn't get in contact with her.

Amy had gone with Simon into Dingo Beach as soon as the road was accessible. The small community had been hit hard, with barely a building undamaged. Cecily's house, which was a small Besser block home, had been spared major damage and there were only a few windows and one side wall to be fixed. Her yard was much the same as everyone's though and it seemed like every tree and plant had either been uprooted or ripped to shreds by the wind.

Cecily's neighbour had made the national news by cutting his way out of his house with a chainsaw. His foresight to take it into the safety of his house saved him from being stuck inside after large trees fell on his house, blocking his way out. The article in the paper was the talk of the small town and although the locals hadn't had much help from the outside world yet they came together and helped each other with what they had.

Dingo Beach was a scene of destruction with roofs torn off and shells of houses left unprotected. Boats washed up onto the shores lay in pieces and debris littered every part of town. The news also revealed the disastrous effects on the islands to the east and in the township of Airlie Beach. Amy had come home full of stories to tell.

They'd celebrated that night with a meal Frankie had cooked while the other two were away. One of the SES groups had dropped some fresh veggies and meat to them and she'd made a tasty stew. They sat at the kitchen table, Charlotte in her highchair and the dogs, including Riley, looking at them through the open back door. The screen doors had blown away and the dogs had tried several times to come back inside to no avail.

They tied Riley up at night, worried that he'd try and go back to his house. Artie was still in hospital and Maureen was staying with family in Proserpine. Simon had been over to their house with the SES crew and helped put a tarp over a section of the roof that had blown away. A couple of outside walls were damaged and Barney had found his way to the downstairs tiled patio area, standing firmly and refusing to move when Simon tried to chase him out.

Simon relayed the story as they sat and ate dinner together. 'He's probably stood there for the last couple of days. You should see the piles of manure. Maureen would have a fit if she could see her beautiful Italian tiles cover in his muck.'

'The SES fellas said Artie's family are coming in tomorrow to clean up,' Amy reported, reaching over for some more bread. 'They won't let Artie out until everything is fixed. Apparently he's threatening to walk out on his crutches if they don't hurry up.'

'He'll be missing his dog and his beers in the afternoon,' Simon added.

Amy sat up and passed them both a plate with some bread she had buttered. 'You know, Dad, I was talking to the SES fellas. I'm old enough to join. They put you through training and then you can help, like at times like this. I'd really love to do it and he said it's great experience for jobs later on once I've left school.'

Simon raised his eyebrows in surprise and glanced at Frankie. She knew what he was thinking. Was this the same girl who had whinged and made their life hell over the last six months? What was going on? 'That sounds like a good idea', Simon responded. 'Do you think you'd like to do that?'

'Yeah, I reckon I would. You get to do your first aid training and gain other certificates. I'm really keen to give it a go. The idea of being a paramedic once I finish school is also something I've been thinking about after talking to the workers. One of them is studying that at the moment. It sounds really interesting.'

'I think it's a fabulous idea,' Frankie said. 'You've got a level head and you were much calmer than I was during it all. I just thought the roof was going to blow away and take the house with it. I was sure we were all going to die.'

Simon chuckled. 'You're a real north-Queenslander now Frankie. Your first cyclone and probably one of the biggest ones we've had in a very long time and from my experience one of the slowest.'

'Those fellas reckon the winds got up to 215 kilometres an hour,' Amy said.

Frankie shuddered. 'I don't really want to go through another one like that. It's alright for you two, you're born and bred up here.'

Amy's voice lowered. 'At least we were all together. Nothing is so bad when you're with each other.'

'That's right,' Simon said. 'The four of us were safe and nothing else matters. The entire house could blow away and every possession in it but as long as you three girls were okay I wasn't worried.'

Amy blinked and Frankie was sure she could see tears in her eyes. Simon leaned over and gave his daughter a hug. 'Now,' he said, 'Let's finish our stew. Frankie I'm sure your cooking has improved.'

She laughed. 'Maybe anything tastes good after those tins of food and dry biscuits.'

Charlotte clapped her hands and looked around at all of them. Her eyes lit up and she squealed with delight as she threw her spoon onto the floor.

'As long as we're all together,' Amy said as she bent down to pick it up. 'Our family, together.'

CHAPTER 20

*J*t was almost like Cyclone Debbie had swept in and blown away not only the trees and buildings but also the old Amy. In her place was a more pleasant teenager who went out of her way to help and involved herself in the day-to-day routines. Charlotte squealed with delight every time she saw her, and they'd all laughed when she pulled Amy's hair and refused to let go.

'You have lovely hair,' Frankie told her. 'It's got a lot more bounce in it now it's not squashed under that beanie.'

'The beanie days are done,' Amy said, gently unwrapping Charlotte's tiny fingers before making sure she had no hair in her hands. 'I've moved on. I had some—as Mr Mackle-Penny would like to call it—reflection time when I wasn't sure you two were going to make it back.'

'That was a bit close that day,' Simon said. 'Well, I'll be honest. I like the new Amy.'

'So do I,' Frankie added. 'And so does Charlotte. She's

lucky to have a big sister and you need to remember that you're just as important to your dad and me as Charlotte is. You and Eli. We're your family.'

'Thanks Frankie, that means a lot to me. I was just so angry with everything and everyone when I arrived here. It felt like no one really cared about me, and everyone had moved on with their own lives that didn't include me.'

They sat together on the beach, the debris from the month before still scattered around them. 'I felt like I had nothing in front of me and nothing behind. The only person I connected with was Jeremy.'

Frankie added in. 'When you're at your age, friends are really important. Jeremy is a good friend. He's like his sister, level-headed but also fun to be with. He does bring out the best in you.'

'He is important, but now I know that you and Dad are also, and ...' she picked up Charlotte and brushed the sand off her clothes. 'Charlie is my sister and she needs me. I was so worried that something was going to happen to her when I sat in the bathroom with her by myself. It was strange, I wasn't worried about myself, just her and the two of you.'

'She loves you,' Frankie said. 'Her little eyes light up as soon as you come in the room.'

Amy bounced Charlotte on her knees. 'Maybe one day I might meet someone like you met Dad. I like seeing how you talk to each other and care for one another. It's a calm place.'

Simon put his arm around her shoulders. 'We have our ups and downs, just like everyone does. No doubt there will be boyfriends and friends that you'll meet. You have a lot going for you.'

'Thanks Dad. I had to nearly die like Dorothy in the Wizard of Oz to realise what I have.'

'Eli and Rose will be here next week to help clean up,' Simon said. 'We'll all be together for the first time in many years.'

Charlotte pulled at Frankie's arm. She was starting to get cranky, it was nearly her sleep time. Amy stood up. 'You two stay here for a little while. I'll put her to bed. I can read her a couple of books.'

They watched as Amy hoisted her onto her hip, Charlotte's head resting on her shoulder. Her little hand reached up and she waved to them, snuggling in as Amy walked up to the house.

Frankie leaned into Simon's shoulder, his arm wrapping around her as he kissed the top of her head. 'Who would ever think that the beanie-loving, surly teenager would transform into a beautiful young lady.'

'Thank goodness,' Frankie said. 'I knew under all that revolting behaviour there was something nice. There had to be, she's your daughter.'

'She's definitely turned the corner, and she is really focussed on becoming a volunteer and then studying to be a paramedic. The change in her is incredible.'

A couple of horses wandered along the beach, stopping for a moment to stare at Frankie and Simon. 'They're Artie's,' Simon said. 'It's going to take months to fix all these fences. They've all been flattened. Jeremy and I are going to give him a hand. At least everyone's okay although I don't know how Maureen is putting up with him not being able to move around much. He'll be driving her crazy.'

'I've made him his favourite fruit cake. I'll take it over

tomorrow and stay for a cuppa. They're good neighbours.' Frankie looked out at the ocean. 'My beautiful sea is not very glittery anymore.' They both stared at the murky churning water that continued to pump onto the beach, each wave bringing in another stick, or piece of debris.

'It will take time to go back to the clear water that we know. And even longer for the area to recover,' Simon said,

'It's going to take us a long time to fix everything up,' Frankie said. 'I can't imagine what it's like over on the islands or in Airlie Beach. The hills and mountains are stripped bare. The cane is flattened. It's like a giant has come through and torn everything from the ground.'

'It is, but we've been through this before. It's part of life up here in the north and we'll recover. The buildings will take months to re-build, the foliage years to grow back. You'll be sick of trying to get the insurance to comply and workman and materials to fix everything up. The locals will work together though and as long as everyone's together and safe, life will go on. You'll see, it will take a while but everything will go back to what it once was.'

Frankie looked up and kissed Simon on the lips. 'As long as I have you and Charlotte, and now we have Amy, I'm happy.'

Seagulls called out as they flew over the waves, their sounds lost in the breeze that gently cooled the air. 'I promise the jewelled sea will return,' Simon said. 'Maybe once everything is restored and looking good, we could have a wedding, right here on the beach.'

She sat up straight. 'How good would that be? A

wedding with our families and friends coming together. A celebration on the beach. Right here where it all started.'

'By the jewel sea,' Simon whispered in her ear.

'Yes, our jewel sea.'

The End

ABOUT THE AUTHOR

Rhonda Forrest is an Australian author who juggles writing and publishing, alongside teaching high school students. She writes captivating contemporary and historical/romance fiction about relationships, family life and social issues, set amidst beautiful and uniquely Australian landscapes.

After bringing up three daughters and traversing several careers, Rhonda went on to teach creative writing, English and history. Her passion for literacy, history and travelling around Australia fuels her novels. Along with her husband, she divides her time between Tamborine Mountain and a century-old cottage with a rambling garden overlooking the waters of the Whitsundays.

Recent novels bring to life the remarkable characters and settings that make up the unique Australian heritage and take the reader on a journey from bush to beach, with steamy romances, riveting history and eclectic characters.

Some books are available in audio and large print. You can also find some titles available in Portuguese, Publisher- Leabhar Books Brazil.

If you enjoyed this book or any of Rhonda's other books, you can make a big difference by writing a review, or leaving a star rating on Amazon, Goodreads or Book-bub. A personal recommendation to family, friends, libraries and book clubs is another great way to share the books with others. You can also follow Rhonda on Face-book, Instagram, Goodreads and Bookbub.

Author's favourite - sample chapters from *Silkworm Secrets* are in the back of this book.

Website - https://www.rhondaforrest.com/

WHITSUNDAY ROMANCE

Enjoy the warmth of a small community in the Whitsundays.

You may never want to leave!

~~~

Love by the Jewel Sea - Book 1

Summer by the Jewel Sea - Book 2

The Lure of the Jewel Sea - Book 3

ALSO BY RHONDA FORREST

OUTBACK QUEENSLAND ROMANCE SERIES

With a cast of eclectic characters and set amidst the rugged outback of Australia, *Outback Queensland Romance Series* will introduce you to stories of friendship, resilience and loving relationships that come together to triumph over obstacles defined by the past.

WE'LL MEET AGAIN TRILOGY

'A dingo howls, a star falls.
Don't worry for me, I'll be home soon.'

We'll Meet Again trilogy is an epic World War II saga that will take you from outback Queensland to the jungles of New Britain, then back to the peaceful hinterland regions of the Sunshine Coast and Tamborine Mountain. Based on actual events that include the invasion of Rabaul, and the tragic sinking of the Montevideo Maru, these are emotional stories of love, survival, and the resilience of the families who waited for their loved ones to return.

*** For your pleasure - Sample chapters from, Book 1 (Elizabeth's Star) are at the back of this book. Happy reading! ***

BINDARRA CREEK ROMANCE

BEYOND THE GATE - Mystery Romance at Bindarra Creek

CHRISTMAS AT FORREST GLEN - A Bindarra Creek
Romance

A MAGICAL SUMMER - A Bindarra Creek Small Town
Christmas Romance

SILKWORM SECRETS SERIES (Book 1 and 2)

Growing up next door to each other in 1960s suburban Brisbane, Ruby and Bobby should have an idyllic childhood. However, Bobby's home life is vastly different than the loving security of Ruby's family, and not even the sanctuary of their shared treehouse set high in a mulberry tree can offer him the safety he needs.

Emotional and layered, *Silkworm Secrets* is a moving story about the secrets children keep, the power of friendship, and a love that overcomes the hardships of the past. *Forever More*, continues the story of Bobby and Ruby and reminds us of the good and bad in people and that a loving family can come in many different forms.

THE SHACK BY THE BAY - Whitsunday Historical Romance

Romantic and purely Australian, *The Shack by the Bay* captures the pristine beauty of the Whitsundays and the wartime memories of older Australians while introducing an eclectic blend of friends and family.

ALL MY HEART - A Tranquil Bay Romance

A small town and school - She only had to last six months.

KICK THE DUST - Contemporary Romance

'If I close my eyes, it's easier to hold onto a memory. When I open them, I think it might really be there in front of me.'

CHAPTERS FROM SILKWORM SECRETS

SAMPLE CHAPTERS

'*he ancient trees with their rough bark wrap around me like silk cocoons. Their solid trunks and tendril roots grip the ground as if to say, I will hold you, I will not let go.*'

CHAPTER 1

There had been great excitement the day the silk-worms first came to the treehouse. Walking knee-deep through the dense covering of ferns and bushes beneath the mulberry tree, Bobby had announced that he had a surprise for Ruby in his satchel. It was dim and cool under the tree, the knotted branches and canopy forming a shady, secluded area, only a few frilly-necked lizards and the occasional brown snake sharing the space with the two of them.

She had tried to get him to stop and open his bag, the suspense almost too much, but he kept walking, determined for once not to let her win.

'Wait, Ruby Rose. Just wait until we climb up and then I'll show you.'

'But what is it? Can't you tell me? I'll die of curiosity.'

Ruby liked to be in charge and know everything. The suspense made her climb erratically, stopping and starting,

continually looking down at Bobby climbing steadily below her.

'Just get up there and I'll show you,' he said.

Standing on her toes, she balanced on the rungs leading up the tree. He noticed the bottoms of her feet, dark purple colours mixed with dirt from the earth below. Her flowery cotton dress was also stained purple from where she had sat on some of the thousands, perhaps millions, of berries that had dropped from the tree during the fruiting season.

Above them, the trail of timber blocks, like steps, wove their way up into the darkest reaches of the tree. Nails that had long ago been hammered into the rough, textured bark held the timber secure, and as they climbed higher, tiny glimpses of the sky became visible; a blue backdrop to the thick branches that reached upwards, their tops covered by the dense canopy of weeping smaller branches and leaves.

Perched amongst the thick foliage of the massive mulberry tree the treehouse was obscured, a safe haven, a place no one else bothered with, tucked away in an over-grown corner of Ruby's backyard. The two best friends considered the spot to be the best place in the world, and its location among other large trees—figs, mangoes and a towering pine tree—provided them with their own secret corner, a safe house with no adults, just the two of them, talking, laughing; conspirators.

'Hurry up.' Ruby used her bossy voice as she held up the canvas for Bobby to enter the treehouse.

Once inside he had reached into his satchel and presented Ruby with a number of pieces of cardboard, all covered in multitudes of silkworm eggs. She was ecstatic and caused him great embarrassment by continually hugging him and then jumping up and down, making the treehouse creak and shake a little.

It had been school holidays and they had watched every day, Ruby recording in her notebook when the tiny, grey eggs stuck to the cardboard had lightened in colour.

Finally the day they had both waited so patiently for: tiny silkworms, hundreds of them, wriggling, squirming and climbing over each other, filling an old school port, safe in their new home.

Although Ruby had only been eight, she was fastidious about keeping records of events that occurred in and around the mulberry tree. She left her small notebook in the treehouse, only removing it when she needed to record major incidents. Today she wrote: *143 healthy silkworms. All eating leaves.*

The silkworms grew quickly, fattening on the never-ending supply of leaves from the mulberry tree that seemed to be at its best, the thick canopy dripping with the heaviness of its foliage and fruit. The job of picking the greenest leaves from the tree and making sure that all the worms were fed had been allotted to Bobby. Bobby's other job was to clean the droppings from the boxes so the silkworms would have enough room to move around.

They had found extra boxes, the original school port now overflowing with fat silkworms that quickly ate through the leaves. Their droppings were bright green, an indication, Ruby told Bobby, that they were happy and healthy.

Once, when Ruby was not around, Bobby had carried the largest container, the school port, down the tree and into his bedroom at home. Plugging in the vacuum cleaner, he had tried—just using the pointy end of the vacuum and not the brush part as he later explained to Ruby—to suck up the droppings and give the container a really good clean.

Ruby had not been impressed and had efficiently recorded in her notebook:

September 24, 1968, 54 large fat silkworms. Now only 12 surviveing.

Bobby and vacum encident.

. . .

Now she needed to make more notes regarding the latest incident. Bobby stood beside her as she recorded in her neat handwriting:

March 4, The accident, 1970.

School port moths, 17 healthy moths, now only 7 surviveing, 2 of those are injared becous of falling from tree.

Bobby and Ruby falling over encident acident.

' What?' Ruby said as she looked up at Bobby, his mouth opening as if to speak.

Perhaps it 's not the best time to point out her spelling mistakes, he thought, as he closed his mouth, instead smiling and shaking his head. ' You're the best club president,' he said, 'and at least we still have some moths, even after the accident yesterday.'

The small girl rolled her eyes at him, an indication that she was not impressed with the situation.

He had long ago decided to ignore Ruby's habit of eye rolling, as well as to go along with most of the ideas she came up with. The time he spent with her was his only sliver of happiness in amongst the misery of home and school, and he would do anything to keep the peace between them, whatever it took to stretch out the time before he had to return home. Even though the happenings of the day before had been calamitous to Ruby, they hadn't even rated in his own list of personal disasters.

Ruby was oblivious to the situation at his house. Although he sometimes longed to tell her what was really happening, he had decided that for now it was better to keep it that way, to keep it all to himself. Just try not to think about it, he told himself.

. . .

CHAPTER 2

The accident had happened the day before, on what had started out as a typical afternoon but had quickly gone wrong; a disastrous chain of events resulting in their moth tally decreasing to just seven.

As usual, they had both rushed home after school and made their way up into the treehouse as quickly as possible. They lay side by side, enjoying the cool of the rough timber flooring in their meeting area.

Bobby was happy to lie still and listen to Ruby as she chattered on about making a new area that she wanted to call the sitting area. Although there were many sections to the treehouse, designated and specified, it was, after all, not such a big structure. They had drawn boundary lines for the different areas on the floor with white chalk, the faint lines invisible in places where their bare feet or bodies had rubbed over them.

Now they sprawled out with their heads in the spying area, feet pushed up against the stump of the activity table, their bodies stretched across three areas—spying, meeting and activities.

Bobby, being the elder and taller of the two, lay contorted, with his knees bent high and his neck twisted slightly so he could fit across the largest flat area of the treehouse. He tried to stretch out his long legs, sinewy from years of school sport and running, before resigning himself to the cramped conditions. Turning his head, he looked through the slits in the timber walls. His intense brown eyes were set deeply, and his tousled dark hair, springy with the Queensland summer humidity, framed his squarish, still boyish face.

Ruby was stretched out fully beside him with her shoulder jammed up against his, her bare feet nowhere near the stump-table that hindered the comfort of the taller Bobby. Conspirators; two sets of eyes flickering back and forth, lying deathly still as if their lives depended on invisibility.

'I told you it was a good idea,' Ruby whispered, indicating the rolled-down canvas across the doorway. ' There's no way anyone can see in now.'

'You're smart for a girl. Sometimes.'

Bobby's chuckle was cut short by the cutting look, a savage glare as the small girl turned towards him, glinting green eyes scowling, her scrunched-up face willing him to remain silent. They stared hard at each other and Bobby concentrated on her face as he counted the biggest freckles, a smattering of cute brown spots across her nose that faded into each other as they ran across the top of her somewhat chubby cheeks. There were a couple of gaps in her teeth where adult incisors had failed to come through quickly enough to mask the fact that she was still young enough to be losing baby teeth.

Knowing better than to tease Ruby about still having teeth like a baby, he kept his quick words to himself rather than incur the wrath and sharp retorts that would flow forth from her; so young but already more than capable of sticking up for herself.

Wavy blonde hair spread out beneath her, so long that it reached below her red cotton shorts. Her thin brown legs were stretched out beside him as she tried to match the length of his own. Ruby didn't like to be far behind Bobby in anything, and she was always measuring her height, telling him that one day they would be the same size.

'But you'll never be as strong as me,' he would say, flexing his muscles, thinking that one day he would have muscles as strong as Popeye in the cartoon pictures.

'My dad says that I can do anything a boy can do,' Ruby said. 'Just because I'm a girl doesn't mean I can't do stuff. He reckons I can do whatever I want, and if I want to be the strongest person, well, I can be.'

'Girls can't do some things that boys can.' Bobby looked at her, suspicious of her confidence and confused about her ideas, so different from what was promoted in his house.

'Of course they can. I can be whatever I want. If I want to be a doctor, well, I can.'

'That's not right. Girls should be nurses or mums.'

'My dad says if I want to be an astronaut like Neil Armstrong then I can be. He says I'm really smart, and when I grow up I can be whatever I want.'

'Bet you can't be a concreter like him.' 'Bet I could.'

'Girls are supposed to get married and have babies. They look after the kids and cook, clean the house.'

'I don't like cooking and cleaning. I hate cleaning the bathtub. I'm going to do something else when I'm grown up.'

'Like what?'

'I'm going to be a lawyer.'

' You mean like on *Homicide*?' he said, referring to the popular television show.

'Yeah, you know, they solve crimes.'

'I thought you weren't allowed to watch those shows. How do you know what a lawyer is when you aren't allowed to watch it?'

'Silkworm secret,' Ruby said. 'If I lie in bed with the door open, I can see the TV screen reflected in the big mirror on the sideboard. My dad's a bit deaf so he has it up pretty loud. I get to see most TV programs, but you can't tell him or Mum.'

'Lawyers are always men.' 'I watch *Matlock Police* too.'

'Your dad would be really angry if he knew you were watching those programs. You'll get in trouble if you get caught.' 'Bobby, I won't get caught. Besides, they're really scary, so most of the time I put my hands over my eyes.'

'You're so lucky that your mum and dad care about you. I wish my parents were like yours. The other day Theresa asked me how you get a new mum and dad. She's tired of all the trouble at home and the way Sally doesn't get looked after properly. I didn't know what to say. I wish I was older, then I'd run away and take them both with me.'

The two best friends stared hard at each other as they talked. It was a game they often played: who could go the longest without blinking. Both blinked sharply, however, when a loud voice bellowed up from under the tree.

'Ruby, you climb down here this minute. I know you're up there. I wasn't born yesterday.' Footsteps scuffed through the thick layer of fallen leaves, moving closer, the voice booming out again. 'You get down here *now*. I've got jobs for you to do and you're not supposed to play until your homework's done.'

The two conspirators, who had no intention of moving or answering, pulled faces at each other, imitating the adult face below.

'Your father will clip you across the ears when you come down and there' ll be no ice cream for you tonight.' Mary, Ruby's mum, waited for a reply. ' You're wasting my time, Ruby. I've got better things to do than look for you. I'm telling you now, though, if you didn't change and you've got mulberry on that school uniform there'll be hell to pay.'

The exasperated voice faded away as Ruby's mum made her way back to the house.

'She's not really mad,' Ruby whispered. 'She just likes to sound like she is, making out she's the boss.'

Bobby looked worried. 'Are you sure your dad won't thrash you?'

The small girl's laughter resounded off the rough timber walls. 'Are you joking? My dad loves me too much. He would never hit me.'

'Does your mum ever hit you?' Bobby was trying to manoeuvre his neck, which was starting to feel like it would be attached sideways on his body permanently.

Ruby's little face scrunched up, her eyes narrowing. 'She loses it sometimes, especially when I keep going on about something. Because I'm more stubborn than her, she knows she can't beat me. I can always tell when she's really mad because her face goes red and her eyes … it's like she's a dragon and there's flames coming out of them, red flames licking out of her green eyes. And sometimes her lips go real thin and mean, like this.' Ruby sat up and gave a demonstration.

' What does she do? Does she use a belt?' ' Worse than that.'

'A cricket bat? A broom handle?' 'Don't be silly.'

'I know,' Bobby said, 'the whippy wire out of the curtains.' His curiosity was aroused as he imaged the horrendous punishment her mother might inflict.

' Way worse.' Ruby loved having Bobby's full attention. 'She goes all quiet, then she starts whispering all the angry things she wants to say to me.'

'You mean she doesn't scream or yell?'

Ruby rolled her eyes. 'No, she goes quieter and quieter, telling me off, saying she's going to tell Dad all the bad things I do.'

'Then what?'

'She snaps off a branch, a thin little branch from the wattle tree out the front. She sort of tests it in the air and then real quick, before I can run away, she twitches me with it.'

'Across your face?'

'No, stupid, across the back of my legs, and it stings like crazy and sometimes it leaves a red mark. If I rub it really hard I can make it stay there until Dad gets home and then I tell him that she whipped me with a thick tree branch.'

'Is that it? A bit of a whack from a wattle twig across your legs?'

' Well, it stings.'

'That's nothing, a little wattle twitch.'

'If I put it on real good and make out it hurts a lot,' Ruby said, 'when I sit with Dad at night he rubs it for me. Then he sort of lectures me, tells me how to get around Mum, how not to annoy her. You know the sort of stuff:

"Your mother loves you, you need to be nice to her, don't bite the hand that feeds you." Dad reckons she's the boss.'

Bobby lay without speaking, staring up at the patchy tin roof. 'Bobby, are you listening to me? Do you reckon your mum's the boss?'

A lengthy silence followed before he spoke. ' There's no way Mum's the boss. You know my old man; you've seen what he's like. He's not kind like your dad.'

'Your dad's always nice to me,' Ruby said, 'and he gives me a little sausage when we go to your meat shop, and sometimes he makes Mum laugh. He always chats to her, tells her she has a pretty dress on, says he can smell her dinners cooking and that she must be the best cook in the street.'

'Ha.'

'Mum says that your dad has done really good to have such a big shop, and Dad reckons your dad is a good butcher giving us the meat cheaper, and he says that your sister Theresa works hard, she does really good at school, and Mum and Dad think you're smart, and your Uncle Mike, well, Mum says, "Fancy having an uncle that knows the prime minister, real high up in the government he is, and he has so much money and—"'

Bobby cut her off, wondering how she could speak for so long without a breath. 'You know things aren't always what they seem to be.'

'Like how?'

'Just … never mind.' He stretched out his stiffening muscles. 'What do you mean? Don't start something and not finish it.' 'I mean sometimes things look good to other people, but

they're only seeing what's on the outside.' ' Well, what's

on the inside?'

'Forget it. I'm going to get your stupid records book so you can write up the tally.' Bobby sat up suddenly, signalling an end to the conversation.

'Hey, I'm the boss.' Ruby grabbed Bobby as he tried to stand up, his long legs wobbly and unsteady after lying cramped and still for so long. 'Just because you're older—'

And that was when, in a split second, it happened: 'the accident' as Ruby liked to refer to it.

It was like watching a slow-motion movie. Ruby gasped out loud as Bobby's legs became tangled, his body twisted, and he lurched unsteadily towards the table in the centre of the treehouse. The piece of fibro that made up the top of the table rested on the stump of a huge branch. Apart from the way the tabletop crumbled a little around the edges from time to time, it made a perfect flat surface for many of their activities.

That day a number of containers were lined up neatly across the table: an old school port with broken hinges, its stickers peeling; two shirt boxes, the colours on their sides faded and blurry; and two smaller shoeboxes. All the lids on the containers had been punched with multiple holes, providing air for the tiny creatures within.

Ruby's eyes widened as Bobby stumbled and fell forward, one arm reaching out to steady himself and stop his face smashing into the boxes on the table. His hand made contact and he grasped wildly at the closest object. Before their eyes, the largest container, the school port, turned over, the lid going one way, and the rest of the port flipping forward and landing upside down in the reading area.

'Shit.' Bobby gathered himself, standing steady, looking from Ruby to the school port.

They both knew. They knew that below that port, which was now lying lidless in the centre of the reading area, were gaps in the timber floor that opened to the ground far below. This was serious. Bobby registered the fact that Ruby hadn't reprimanded him for swearing; rule number five on the list of Silkworm Club rules.

Ruby crawled slowly over to the port and waited for Bobby. Together they lifted it, cautiously moving it straight up and not sliding it, or allowing it to have any more contact with the floor than necessary.

'Uh-oh.'Bobby pursed his lips and waited for Ruby's response. 'They've nearly all fallen through the gaps,' Ruby said. 'They won't live, they can't fly.' Her voice was shaky as she carefully tried to pick up the contents that had fallen from the container. Bobby pressed his face to the openings between the floorboards, one eye closed, trying to spy any survivors of the fall. Ruby's voice took on the steadiness and authority of the Silkworm Club president. 'I'll pick these ones up. Can you please go down and see if you can find any on the ground?'

She scooped up the mulberry leaves scattered on the floor, a few silkworm moths gripping to their surface, their delicate wings flapping wildly, their eyebrows furrowed. 'It looks like there are about five here. That means twelve are missing. This morning there were seventeen.Hurry up, Bobby, they only live for a few days so we need to find them and put them back in the box. Then they can lay their eggs.'

As usual, Bobby followed her instructions. Even though he was older by three years, Ruby was the club president, and besides, she was good at organising every-thing and everybody. It was easier to just follow her directions and do what he was told.

He scrambled down the tree trunk, hanging onto the timber steps and hand guides that wound their way down to the ground. The thought of looking for white moths that had probably drifted off on the wind made him smile. He knew that the heavy leaf litter and dense ferns growing wild under the tree would envelop and hide a free-falling silkworm moth that had no sense of surviving in the wild.

But he would try; he would do anything to please Ruby because she was, after all, his best friend.

CHAPTER 3

Dad says you've just got to get on with stuff,' Ruby said as she tidied the treehouse. 'Step forward and don't cry over spilt milk. I' ll bring a mat up and put it over the gaps in the floor.'

The boxes on the table were now lined up straight. Everything had to be in its place and she cast her eyes over the timber boxes, squinted and then rolled her eyes when she noticed the ice-cream tin with a few large mouldy mulberries left in it. 'Got it.' Bobby tipped the few remaining mulberries out the window, replacing the container in its correct position on the shelf. Amused at how neat she had to have everything, he watched her move the crate chairs so they were even and straight.

They both ran their hands over the boxes that were full of cocoons. When the moths hatched, they would hopefully add to their now decreased tally.

'See you in the morning,' Ruby said to the silkworms.

Bobby held up the canvas for her as they made their way out of the treehouse and into the real world below.

When they reached the bottom of the tree they sat for a while, balancing on the huge protruding roots that were covered in the same rough bark as the trunk; sections of the roots smooth however, due to the continuous movement of bare feet across them over the years.

'I have to go in,' Ruby said eventually. 'It's nearly night. Even Dad will go mad if I come in after dark.'

'I better go home, too. I still have to do all my jobs before Dad gets home. I'm sorry about the moths, Ruby Rose.'

'Best friends don't get mad with each other. It was sort of my fault, too.'

Emerging from the cover of the trees, they turned in the direction of their houses, both looking up at the horizon as the fading light threw an orange hue over the backyard. Ruby saw the light flick on over the back veranda and knew her dad would be starting to look at the clock, wondering if he should call her in to clean up before dinner.

'See you tomorrow.' Bobby sounded despondent, sad.

He never wants to go home, Ruby thought. He must really like the silkworms, and me, better than his own family.

The darkening light separated them, the clicking of the side gate indicating that Bobby was in his own yard.

Sure enough, Ruby's dad Francis was sitting out on the back steps, his work boots and socks kicked off to the side as he enjoyed a smoke in the balmy evening light. She ran towards him, her small legs going, as her dad would say at a million miles an hour. Placing his cigarette down on the brick stairs beside him, he held both arms out as she jumped onto him. Chubby arms wrapped around his neck, her kisses smothering his face.

'My Ruby Rose, my little mulberry fairy,' he said, squeezing her tightly, his face nuzzling into her blonde wavy hair.

'I'm never going to let go of you.' Ruby clung to him, her mulberry-stained face squashed into the hairs on his chest, her legs drawn up so she could nestle in, snug and secure.

' What have you been up to today, little one?' He moved her to one side so he could puff on his cigarette.

'Dad, Dad, you'll never believe what happ—'

Her mum's voice interrupted them. 'Right, you two, the pair of you, grubs. One covered in mulberry, the other in concrete dust. You need to clean up before you come in for dinner. Stop your story right now, Ruby. We'll listen while we have dinner and then I'll decide if you get dessert.'

Ruby recalled the earlier incident, when her mother was looking for her, calling out. It seemed so insignificant now. Wait until she told them about the moths, and how Bobby had rescued two of them, then surely she would get dessert.

Francis picked her up and she wrapped herself around the front of him, her arms around his neck and her legs wrapped around his waist. They looked at each other and laughed together.

Ruby's mum put on her cranky voice. 'Clean up, both of you, or else there'll be no dinner for either of you.'

Steam rose from the hot water as Ruby bathed, only her head above the water as she lay back in the old claw-foot bath. She loved the bathtub. It was deep enough for her to float in, and the warm water closed in over her, softening the mud and mulberry stains. Her dad would be in the outside shower now, scrubbing hard, removing the dried concrete and dust, the remnants of a day of hard work. She knew he would wait until she had run the bath water, letting her get the hot water first in case it ran out. After he finished, her mum would send him in to get Ruby moving.

She hated getting out of the tub. Instead, she always drew out her time, leaving it until the last moment to take the small scrubbing brush from the wire basket hanging on the wall. Then she would scrub as hard as she could, removing all of the dirt and stains from her hands and feet. She knew her mum would inspect her cleanliness, and if she had missed any marks, Ruby would have to use the bucket and cold water outside to finish off after dinner.

The door rattled as her dad banged on it. 'Hurry up, dinner's out.'

Ruby emerged scrubbed and refreshed. Her dad hugged her, one hand ruffling her hair, both revelling in the freshness of feeling clean.

The three of them sat around the small dining-room table and ate their evening meal, her mum smiling and relaxed now, her dad talking about his day. It was the usual steak and mash, carrots, and of course the greens—beans and peas. This was their favourite time of the day. It was quiet, just the family, all tucked up together, ready to chat and catch up with what each other had done during the day.

Her dad beamed at both of them. 'Righto, Ruby Rose, now tell us what exciting things you did today.'

***

Silkworm Secrets - Dark Secrets from a Distant Past